Tales from the

Camel Trail

Monday

Pearl Davey

A Catalogue record for this book is available from the
British Library

ISBN: 978-0-9572785-0-9

Cover design by Jonathan Cooksley

Edited by Judi Hunter

Typeset by John Dickinson

Printed and bound in Great Britain by
TJ International Ltd, Padstow

To my seven precious stars.
You are all different sizes,
but you all shine equally bright.

Contents

Chapter 1

Cousins reunited

"Get a move on, Tank!" Red shouted up the stairs. Red was so excited. He loved meeting up with his cousins and, right now, they were on the night train from Reading with Auntie Angela. The train was due to arrive at Bodmin in half an hour and, as always, the Evans family was running behind.

Red had been waiting downstairs for ages. Red was a carefree, twelve year old who took great pride in being the quickest in the household to get ready, taking only seconds to put on his favourite T-shirt and shorts each morning. Red had been in and out of the bathroom in an instant too. He barely ever checked his appearance in the mirror; it didn't matter to him what he looked like. Mum would sometimes nag him to brush his mop of fiery-red curls but, in Red's opinion, that was just wasting precious play time.

Tank, on the other hand, was never in

a rush in the morning. He would take such a long time getting ready, as he was far too easily distracted by the toys in his bedroom. Tank appeared at the top of the stairs, proudly holding the Lego™ truck he had just painstakingly made, and not at all worried that he was still wearing his pyjamas.

"Great!" said Red sarcastically. "We are going to be so late, we will miss the train coming in. I don't believe you, Tank. Get your clothes on right now!"

Red went into the lounge where Mum was frantically whizzing around with a duster in one hand and scooping up jumpers with the other. Tank's discarded jumpers had been scattered about the living room for days, possibly weeks! However, today, Mum wanted the house looking especially clean for the arrival of Red's cousins. Red thought Mum need not bother, because all that his cousins would see when they entered the house would be the cardboard boxes spilling over with junk and bric-a-brac, which littered the hall, lounge and dining room. Not to mention the obstacle course on the upstairs landing!

Mum must have heard Red enter the lounge because, without even turning around, she asked, "Where on earth is your Dad?"

Red assumed it was a rhetorical question, as Mum knew full well that Dad had gone out for his early morning cycle ride on the Camel Trail, and would probably return about a minute before they were due to leave for the station. Dad was so laid back like that. Red, too, was well aware that he had absolutely nothing to gain from answering the question. He feared he may even get roped into putting Tank's jumpers away. He was just about to sidle quietly out of the room when Dad came running in.

"All aboard," Dad announced, whilst waving the van keys in the air.

Tank suddenly appeared in the lounge – dressed. "Come on then everyone," he said, as he beckoned Mum, Dad and Red to the front door, like a conductor inviting waiting passengers to board the bus. Tank smiled, and then the rest of the Evans family smiled and laughed.

Red was always amazed at how Tank, a

feisty and confident eight year old, managed to avoid being told off. He could easily win Mum and Dad over by smiling his way out of trouble. He just had the cutest and cheekiest grin, helped along by his freckled nose and dimpled cheeks. You could not help but love Tank.

Tank's real name was Dylan. He had started rugby a couple of years ago and had instantly been given the name 'Tank' on the pitch. His coach had said he was such a solid player, knocking down any opponent who dared to get in his way, just like an army tank going through a battlefield. His rugby nickname then just stuck at home. Mum and Dad had joked that it was such a fitting name anyway, as they could always work out where Tank had been due to the devastating trail of destruction he left behind!

Tank was pleased he was no longer known as Dylan and that, like his brother, he too had a nickname. Red had in fact been christened Jed. However, somehow Jed became known as Red.

It all started when Jed was about five and one of his friends called him Red at school. Jed had loved the name so much, and had told Mum and Dad that Red suited him better than Jed because of his fiery-red hair. Mum and Dad had thought he was joking at first, however, that particular discussion was seven years ago and Mum and Dad cannot remember the last time they called him Jed.

The Evans family jumped in the van and set off for Bodmin. Dad reckoned that if the traffic was on their side, they could still get there in time to see the train arrive in the station.

Red could tell Mum was excited about seeing the girls as she was singing along to the radio, only stopping now and again to remind Dad to avoid certain roads, even though there was little traffic about this Sunday morning. Dad just nodded. Knowing Dad, he probably wasn't listening. Mum would often tell Dad things and then ask him to repeat her last sentence. Sometimes he got it right but, more often than not, Dad would not have a clue what Mum had just said. Mum would always just laugh it off, joking that Dad never listened. Mum said Red and Tank were the same, all of them in a world of their own!

Red was so happy. Playing with Tank all day on the Trail in the school holidays was when he was happiest, and having his cousins around to join in the fun was even better. He was always daydreaming about the different adventures they'd had and still planned to have. Unprompted, Red joined Mum in singing the chorus of 'Things Can Only Get Better' as loud as possible.

"We're here!" shouted Tank, as the van pulled into Station Road. "The train is coming, stop here Dad, please, so we can get out."

Dad pulled over to allow the boys to jump out. Tank did not even bother to close the van door behind him; he just fled off towards the platform, nearly running into a man and his dog as he did so. Red sighed and made his way to the other side of the van to close Tank's door for him. That was just typical of Tank. Tank had been the last one ready at home but, somehow, seemed to be the first one in line waiting for the girls.

Red got to the platform just as the train stopped. Tank was jumping up and down with excitement. Red was equally excited and he, too, could not help but jump up and down with delight when he saw his cousins step down on to the platform.

Lilly and Sophie ran towards the boys. Lilly was as tall as Red now, despite being a year younger.

"Hi, Tiger," said both boys together. Lilly was called Tiger by the Evans family.

Last summer, the girls had spent practically most of the school holidays in Cornwall with the boys. During their adventures, both Lilly and Sophie had suggested the four of them have a gang name. Red and Tank were not so sure and thought a gang name for the four of them would not be at all cool. Tank had come up with the idea that, instead, it would be more fun, and less embarrassing for him, of course, if the girls assumed code names for when they came to Cornwall. The girls were delighted when Tank had suggested this and could not wait to be known by their special names. Lilly was called Tiger, after the plant Tiger Lily.

Sophie's alias was Fudge. Tank had suggested this because of the golden, fudge-like colour of Sophie's hair. Somehow the name suited her. Fudge was a very bright and fun seven year old. Nothing fazed her and, despite having a small frame and angelic looks, she was in fact a real tomboy. She loved messing around with the boys and would get most upset if anyone dared to suggest she could not keep up with either Red or Tank.

Tiger loved her name too, although it did not seem quite as fitting. Tiger was graceful, gentle and very caring. She did not seem to have an angry bone in her body, and she had a natural ability to diffuse arguments between others. Somehow, the four children, with all of their different characteristics, just fitted together perfectly.

As the children greeted each other, Mum made her way to Auntie Angela, who had just got down from the train with all the bags.

"How long are the girls staying?" Red heard mum say jokingly to Auntie Angela, who was surrounded by cases. They hugged for what seemed like ages to the children.

Mum and Auntie Angela were incredibly close and both were terribly upset that Auntie Angela did not have any time to stay. She was in fact going back on the next train to Reading, due to leave in fifteen minutes, having journeyed all the way with the girls just to see their safe handover. Auntie Angela had to get back to her job as an Agency Nurse to cover other people's holidays. Her job was the reason why Tiger and Fudge spent most of their school holidays with their cousins in Cornwall. The girls were used to being away from home, however, Mum and Tiger were having to comfort Fudge as Auntie Angela's train slowly pulled away from the station.

"Keep it together, Fudge," said Dad. "I need you to be strong for the surprise I have in store for you."

Fudge's frown quickly disappeared and, desperate to know what was planned, she ran over to her uncle and gave him a big cuddle. "Tell me now, please Uncle Dave, what is it?"

Dad was great with surprises. Red and Tank thought their dad was the best dad ever. He would encourage the boys to have fun and take risks. Dad always wanted to hear every last detail of their adventures too. Mum often said Dad was a big kid at heart and that he would prefer to be joining in with the boys' adventures rather than going to work.

Fudge stayed with the others while Dad led Mum a few steps away and then whispered something in her ear. The children could see that Mum did not seem particularly happy.

"Oh no, Dave!" said Mum as she stepped back from Dad and gave him one of her 'you've been naughty looks' that Red and Tank knew only too well. "What will Angela say when she finds out? We're supposed to be looking after the girls. I'm not even going to be able to tell her that we drove them home safely!"

Dad was not listening though, or was at least pretending not to, as he led the children to the back of the van and then flung open the rear doors.

"For some reason, I packed all four bikes so you kids can cycle home on the Trail," said Dad, grinning.

"Brilliant, thanks Uncle Dave," squealed Fudge with excitement.

"Please Auntie Susan, please can we cycle home with the boys?" pleaded Tiger.

Mum could not help but break into a smile. When Dad had a plan it would usually go ahead no matter how much Mum argued against it. Mum was reminded that Dad's spontaneity was what she loved about him. "Expect the unexpected with me," he would always say. Red and Tank were ecstatic, as it meant they could have fun on the Trail on the way home rather than be stuck in the van, and Tiger and Fudge longed to stretch their legs after their train journey.

Dad went over to Red and whispered something in his ear. Dad also discretely placed something in the little chest pocket of Red's T-shirt.

"Tell me, tell me too," Tank begged.

"Your brother will tell you all in good time," replied Dad. That was typical of Dad. He always had something up his sleeve. "Come on kids, let me introduce you to Lancelot," he said, winking at Red.

"Who's Lancelot?" asked Tank.

"Wait and see," was all Dad would say in reply.

Mum, Dad and Red helped carry all four bikes over the foot bridge to the platform on the other side of the track. Just as they had done so, the children's attention was grabbed by a very loud 'chugging' sound followed by some hissing and blowing.

"Wow," said all of the children as they saw a fantastic bright red and green steam train emerge through the trees.

"Look!" shouted Fudge, as she pointed to the giant plume of smoke bursting into the sky from the chimney. "Uncle Dave, it's a real steam train," she squealed as she tugged at her uncle's shirt.

"Cool," said Tank, moving a little nearer to the edge of the platform to get an even better view as the train pulled up alongside them.

It was a superb train, beautifully polished and glistening in the morning sun. Behind the engine were five bottle-green carriages. Everyone on the platform had stopped to admire the train and to take photographs.

"A mighty fine train, isn't it?" said Dad.

"Look, Dad, it's called Lancelot!" Tank cried out as he saw the highly-polished brass nameplate on the side of the train. "You just said Lancelot. Is this what you meant?" asked Tank.

Dad gave Tank a congratulatory pat on the head for working out the surprise.

"That's right, Tank," said Dad. "This is Lancelot and he is taking the four of you to Boscarne Junction. You can all cycle home safely on the Trail from there. So, kids, this is where Mum and I leave you, where your adventure starts."

Tank, Tiger and Fudge ran excitedly to the first carriage behind the engine.

"This one's mine," said Tank as he threw himself into the seat facing the engine.

Tiger and Fudge watched from the window as Red and Dad put the bikes in the middle carriage where there was a large storage rack to keep them secure. Dad then spoke with the Guard, who very kindly agreed to help the children and their bikes off at Boscarne Junction. Mum felt much better now Dad had done that, although Dad had been trying to convince Mum that it was not possible for the children to get lost in any event as the steam train would take the children straight to the Camel Trail.

"We're off," announced Red, as he saw the Guard waving a green flag on the platform, followed by the piercing shrill of a whistle.

Lancelot slowly pulled away from the station, letting out a superb huffing and puffing noise as the engine picked up speed. The smoke billowed up into the air and, now and again, some of the smoke would waft past the open window of the train door and into the carriage. Tiger and Fudge were still stood at the window, waving goodbye to their uncle and aunt, when the train entered a wooded valley. Within seconds, all the girls could see was a mass of trees, the station platform was now out of sight. Tiger and Fudge excitedly took their seats in the carriage, immediately opposite the boys.

The children felt very grown up indeed to be on the train without an adult accompanying them. Red felt especially responsible when the Ticket Collector entered their carriage and approached him.

14

"Tickets please, Sir," said the Ticket Collector to Red.

Dressed in a very smart waistcoat and brass-buttoned jacket, he told the children it was an actual Guard's uniform from the 1940s. Red confidently produced the train tickets from his T-shirt pocket, which Dad had put there earlier. The Ticket Collector glanced at them. He did not punch a hole in them as he should have done, as Fudge asked him not to. Fudge desperately wanted the tickets to be perfectly intact for her to show to her school teacher during class show-and-tell time. Red handed the tickets to Fudge to keep them and she carefully placed them in her purse, which she then put back in her dress pocket.

The children continued the rest of the journey in silence, quietly taking in the sights and sounds of this very special train ride. The seats were very different from the multicoloured bucket-type seats the girls had just travelled in from Reading. These were plump, cushioned seats covered in a deep red, velvety material and surrounded by wooden casing. It was very luxurious and the shiny metal fittings on the wooden panelled doors looked ever so grand. The children listened to the clack, clack, clacking tune made by the wheels on the track and the huffing and puffing of the engine. At one point, the train stopped and the children actually saw the shiny engine drive past the train. The engine was then put at the back of the train. The four of them were delighted as they got to travel both forwards and backwards without even having to change seats!

As the train started to slow down, Red knew they were approaching Boscarne Junction. He told the others to get ready to get off soon, but none of them wanted the journey to end.

"I haven't been on a steam train before," said Fudge. "It really feels like we have gone back in time." Everyone agreed.

The Guard kindly saw the children and their bicycles safely off the train.

"Have fun and enjoy the rest of your holiday," he said, waving the children off towards the Trail.

"We will. I just know we will," said Red. It felt like their adventures had only just begun.

Chapter 2

Dodgy dealings!

Cycling through the Camel Valley, just the four of them, was such a great start to the holiday. The girls loved the freedom they had in Cornwall. The Camel Trail was their favourite place of all. Whilst they loved going to the beach, being able to explore the Trail with Red and Tank was so much more fun.

The four of them had practically lived on the disused railway line last summer. They had yet to properly explore the nearby towns of Padstow and Bodmin though, as they never seemed to make it to either end of the Trail with enough time to look around. The children just had far too much fun going 'off Trail' along the way, either exploring the adjoining woodland, river banks or quiet little beaches that the other cyclists and walkers just seemed to pass by.

The children were about half way home along the Trail when Red shouted out, "Hey, everyone, time to stop in a moment!"

"What is it?" asked Tank. "Tell us, Red," he said, wondering if this was something else to do with what Dad had whispered to Red at the station. Red did not answer but, shortly after, he stopped and got off his bike. It was near to one of the boys' favourite spots. Red left his bike on the side of the Trail and walked into the woodland. The three followed him the short distance to their very own rope swing, hidden away from the Trail.

Dad had found the rope swing a couple of years ago purely by accident during a game of hide-and-seek. Whilst Dad and the boys had been overjoyed, Mum was worried it would not be safe. Mum had insisted Dad give it a trial run that day, a safety check before the boys got on it. In fact, Dad had given it an exceptionally long trial run and Mum had wondered if it was due to him actually having too much fun to get off. Fortunately for the boys though, the swing had withstood the thorough testing and it soon became their favourite hideout.

The boys called it their 'secret swing' as there was never anyone else playing on it.

Mum and Dad thought it was because it was hidden away, but Red and Tank were sure it was because 'Mad Meeks' lived just a short distance away from the swing and all the other children were probably too scared of him to play there.

Mad Meeks was the name Red and Tank had given to the grumpy old man who lived at River View Cottage, a little cottage by the river on the Trail, just a few hundred metres away from the rope swing. Red and Tank had experienced many scary encounters with Mad Meeks just outside his home.

The boys were frightened of Mad Meeks, and the signs he had put up outside to warn people away made him even scarier. There were two wooden signs that read 'DANGER – KEEP AWAY' and 'PRIVATE' in white paint. It just so happened that the river bank right next to Mad Meeks' front gate was the best place on the Trail for Red and Tank to play pooh sticks. They simply could not resist stopping to play there, as the swirling water at that section of the river helped the sticks 'whoosh' along past the large tree roots that jutted out from the river bank. It also helped that the boys could stand right on the edge of the wooded bank to race their sticks, not to mention the endless supply of twigs and sticks at that spot.

Often, though, their game would come to an abrupt end with Mad Meeks loudly tapping his walking stick on the front window of his cottage, whilst frantically waving the boys away with his other hand. Sometimes, Mad Meeks would appear outside the front of his cottage shouting at the boys to "get away" and "stay away". Fortunately, the boys always managed to get away safely, either sprinting or pedalling as fast as they could away from him.

Yet, here, at their secret swing, Red and Tank felt safe out of view of Mad Meeks' cottage. Just as Tank was about to pull himself up on the swing, Red shouted, "Stop!" so loudly it made Tank jump. Tiger and Fudge couldn't help but laugh.

"What happened to ladies first, Tank?" Red asked.

Fudge quickly added, "Yes, Tank. It's shivery, have you not heard?" Fudge was funny without trying to be. She always knew what she meant to say, but the long words she tried to use often came out a little bit wrong.

"You mean chivalry, not shivery, Fudge!" Tiger corrected.

Fudge went a little red with embarrassment before joining in with the others laughing. Tank duly stood aside and helped Fudge get on to the swing. He also offered to give her a gentle push, but Fudge refused, knowing only too well that Tank would not be able to restrain himself. Tank would no doubt make the swing go as high as possible and Fudge was just not prepared to be scared to death on her first afternoon.

"Here we are," said Red, proudly producing four hot steak pasties.

"No way! How did you manage that?" Tank quizzed Red.

"Thanks to Dad," answered Red.

Dad was such a fantastic planner. He often cycled the Trail for his exercise in the mornings. Today, knowing that he planned for the children to cycle home from the station, Dad had bought some fresh pasties in Wadebridge as soon as the pasty shop opened. On his cycle ride, he had stopped to hide them by the rope swing. He had even carefully planned the taking of the cloth to wrap them in so they had kept beautifully hot.

"Thank you, Uncle Dave," said Tiger, holding her pasty up to the sky. "What a treat. A Cornish pasty for our first meal here."

After the children had devoured every last morsel of their pasties, they spent a couple of hours playing on the rope swing, combining this with a game of hide-and-seek. The person swinging would give the others five minutes to hide. Somehow, Tank was always found first. Tank thought it most unfair. However, the other three had told him it was simply because he was rubbish at hiding. There would always be some part of his body sticking out of the undergrowth. Either that or the bushes would be rustling, as Tank found it hard to sit still for long.

After all the fun and games, the children started to make their way back home. Back on their bicycles on the Trail, Tank led the way as they cycled towards Mad Meeks' cottage. Red was quite a way behind the other three, bringing up the rear and enjoying

the views. As Tank approached Mad Meeks',
he leant forward and pedalled furiously past
the cottage, leaving Tiger and Fudge quite
a distance behind him. The girls had in fact
slowed down to admire the back garden,
which was bordered from the Trail by a dry
stone wall. It was just low enough for Fudge
to see over if she stood up out of the saddle
as she cycled by.

"Look, Tiger. See all those beautiful
flowers," she said. "What fantastic colours.
I think they are lilies, aren't they?"

Tiger agreed with Fudge that they were
beautiful. Fudge was right too, they were
mostly lilies. Tiger and Fudge had often
stopped to look at Mad Meeks' back garden
as it was one of the prettiest gardens they
had ever seen. Both girls loved flowers and
collecting them to press. They could have
spent hours looking around his borders and
at all the different plants he grew. There were
also about six or seven greenhouses dotted
about the garden. They, too, were full of all
sorts of beautiful and exotic-looking plants
and flowers.

The girls turned around and could see

Red half-heartedly pedalling towards them. Red was approaching Mad Meeks' cottage incredibly slowly, as he was busy daydreaming about what they could all get up to this week. It was always fun when Tiger and Fudge came to stay.

"Fancy a quick game of pooh sticks?" Red shouted to the girls as he jumped off his bicycle in front of Mad Meeks' cottage and gestured for them to make their way back towards him. The girls quickly turned their bicycles around and made their way back to Red.

"I don't think we should," said Tiger. "Tank has cycled on. He went so fast."

Red looked ahead and could just about make out Tank waiting on the verge quite a distance up the Trail. As Red turned back towards the river bank, his attention was drawn to the little driveway at the side of the cottage.

"Look, girls," Red whispered to Tiger and Fudge.

"Gosh, yes, it is one of those conversionables that Mummy likes," said Fudge.

"You mean convertible, Fudge and, no, not the car, look at that really tall man," Red whispered to the girls. "He is handing over money to Mad Meeks. Gosh, it looks like an awful lot of money."

All three children had now stopped and were staring, quietly watching as Mad Meeks put the pile of notes into his jacket pocket. The tall man quickly put a box in the boot of his car before slamming it shut. He then darted around to the front of his car and literally threw himself into the driver's seat. The car engine then started and, as Mad Meeks turned to walk to his door, he caught sight of the three children who were staring right at him.

"Quickly, come on!" shouted Red and, without any hesitation, the three of them frantically cycled away towards Tank, who was still waiting further up the Trail next to his bicycle.

"What have you been doing?" asked Tank as they sped towards him, all of them incredibly out of breath.

"You won't believe it!" said Red. "We have just seen something very strange at

Mad Meeks'. A very, very tall man in a red convertible has just paid Mad Meeks a load of money for something in a box, which the tall man then stashed away in his boot. Just as the tall man was about to speed away, Mad Meeks spotted us watching. Gosh, he looked so angry when he saw that we had seen."

"We only just got away," said Fudge.

"It was close," said Tiger. "But what if they come after us now, to ask why we were spying on them? What if the tall man is driving this way now? What if they come to your house, Red? What if...?"

"Stop it, Tiger," interrupted Red. "They don't know where we live and we haven't done anything wrong. Besides, we can get off the Trail going up the short cut Tank and I discovered a couple of weeks ago. It is a fantastic hidden tunnel. We don't think anybody else knows about it."

"Yeah, it is awesome. Wait till you see it, girls," said Tank.

Tiger and Fudge followed Red and Tank a little further up the Trail until they were nearly home. The girls knew they were near because they could see Tanner's Farm in the distance, on the brow of the hill to their right on the north side of the river. The children had visited there last summer to buy fresh eggs and milk for their Auntie Susan. Mrs Tanner had loved the children visiting and had given them each a homemade scone, piled high with jam and clotted cream, to eat on their way home. The girls so hoped they would get to visit the farm this week.

Red told everyone to quickly get off their bikes and follow him off the Trail down towards the river. The children did as Red had asked, Red leading the way first to the river bank and then towards town for about fifteen paces until he abruptly stopped. The children watched as Red then took a large handful of ivy and moved the big clump to one side, revealing a large tunnel entrance.

Tiger was not impressed. "It looks very dark and scary. I don't like the look of it at all."

"It's fine, Tiger, trust us," said Red. "Tank and I found the tunnel when we were playing hide-and-seek a couple of weeks ago and we have been in it every day since. It is perfectly safe. There is nothing to worry about, Tiger. It just looks a little dark for the first bit of the tunnel. Once you are half way in, you can see the light coming from the other side. Seriously, when you have been in once you will see what we mean."

Fudge looked far more enthusiastic than Tiger, "Where does it go to?" she asked.

"Under the Trail and up towards our house," replied Tank.

"You can't tell a soul about it, this is our top-secret hideout," Red insisted. "Not even Dad knows about it. Tank and I figured that it would be more fun that way. We are sure no one else knows about it at all as both entrances are well off the Trail. We know exactly how to find the tunnel entrance though as this one is right opposite Tanner's Farm on the hill. Come on and we'll show you where it goes."

No sooner had Red finished speaking, he entered the tunnel, it being just wide enough for him to push his bicycle alongside.

"You will need to stoop just a little, Tiger, so you don't bang your head!" he shouted behind him.

However, Fudge and Tank had already followed Red in and Tiger was still waiting outside the tunnel entrance.

"Wait, don't leave me!" screamed Tiger. "I want to go the normal way home."

"Follow us or you'll have to go up over the Trail!" shouted Tank from inside the tunnel.

"I'm not coming!" Tiger shouted back.

"Your choice, but look out in case that man is waiting for you!" joked Tank.

Tiger did not wait any longer. She quickly entered the tunnel. The others knew that she had eventually decided to follow them as her loud scream echoed up towards them.

"Sssshhhhhh," said Red, his response echoing back down the tunnel towards Tiger. "We don't want anyone to hear us."

All four of them were soon at the top and exiting the tunnel. Fudge was jumping up and down, pleading with the boys to do it again. Tiger was not at all keen to go back in quite so soon, but she accepted that it had not been half as bad as she had first thought on entering the tunnel. Tiger and

Fudge agreed that, although it was cold and probably home to many different creepy crawlies, the fact that it was the boys' secret tunnel made it ever so exciting.

The four of them made their way up the path towards Red and Tank's house in the nearby hamlet.

"What a great start to the holiday," said Fudge.

"Action packed as always!" said Tiger, still worrying a little about the incident with Mad Meeks and the tall man.

However, they all agreed that it was great to be together again. What would tomorrow bring?

Chapter 3

What a find!

Later that evening, having devoured Mum's homemade cottage pie and creamy rice pudding, the children were discussing their plans for the next day.

Both Red and Fudge wanted to cycle to Padstow to spend the day crabbing. Tank did not want to venture quite so far, suggesting they spot birds from the hide and perhaps have a dip in the river when they needed to cool down. Tiger did not say much other than she was happy to do what the others wanted, and that she did not wish to get her hair wet quite so soon in the holidays.

As much as Tiger liked swimming, it really was a chore having to wash her mass of cascading brown curls. Not only that, but she had only just been to the hairdresser the day she travelled down. She really did not want to waste the money Mummy had spent on her hair appointment and, besides, it really had been blow-dried into the nicest style ever, so she wanted to keep it looking like it did for as long as possible.

One thing the children had agreed on was that Mad Meeks was a scary man and they did not want to bump into him tomorrow. However, they were all a little curious about what he had been involved in today.

"Shouldn't we tell Auntie Susan about what happened with Mad Meeks today, just in case?" asked Tiger.

"Just in case what?" replied Red. "Nothing is going to happen. We don't quite know what he was up to and what is the point of telling Mum and Dad anyway? They just say he is a lonely old man who is probably used to peace and quiet. They have never been bothered when we have told them how much he has shouted at us in the past. They usually just say we probably make too much noise outside his house and perhaps we disturb him napping. Mum always says that Tank is miserable and grumpy when he is rudely awoken and that Mad Meeks is probably the same. Besides, he didn't actually shout at us today, did he?"

"Yes, but he stared right at us, as if he wanted to come and get us," said Fudge. "Because we saw him doing something ilregal."

"Illegal, Fudge," corrected Tiger. "Anyway, we don't know enough about what he was doing to know if it was illegal."

"It definitely looked dodgy to me," said Red. "Perhaps Tank is right and we should go to the bird hide and then the rope swing tomorrow. That way, we can have a quick look at Mad Meeks' as we cycle by. Who knows? We could find out a bit more."

After what seemed like ages discussing their plans, the four of them decided to go to the bird hide and the swing. Tank was really pleased and made no attempt to hide his smirk. Somehow, he had managed to persuade both Red and Fudge to change their minds. Tiger, too, had even gone along with the decision, although she would watch the others from the river bank if they went for a swim. Also, she was adamant she would be cycling past Mad Meeks' cottage at full speed, even if the others wanted to slow down and investigate a little.

—∞∞∞—

Mum hurried into the room almost knocking over one of the boxes.

"Is everything all right, Auntie Susan?" asked Fudge politely.

Mum had already started to empty one of the boxes on to the lounge floor before answering Fudge. "I need to find the china butter dish that is in one of these boxes," she said. "I have to take it to the shop, as I told one of my customers about the daisy pattern on it. They are popping in tomorrow to have a look, as they are very interested in buying it."

Mum and Dad own an antiques and bric-a-brac shop in town called 'This'n'that'. It is an 'Aladdin's Cave', with every single nook and cranny of the two-floored timber building crammed with jewellery, outfits, books, furniture and a vast array of other antiques and collectibles.

Each day, Mum and Dad carefully add new stock to the already overflowing cabinets and shelves from different pieces they pick up from house clearances and jumble sales. The only problem they have is not being able to house all the stock in the tiny stockroom at 'This'n'that'. That is why Mum and Dad joke that their beautiful family home now resembles a warehouse because of the cardboard boxes scattered around the different rooms. The fifth bedroom, the 'box room', is in fact just that, a room full of boxes! Red and Tank don't seem to mind at all though and have successfully mastered the art of manoeuvring around the cardboard boxes at home.

However, Tank has not been quite so successful at making his way around the shop. Mum regularly has to remind Tank of the day that he managed to break five valuable items in the shop simply by swinging his school bag on to his shoulder. In fact, Tank has not been allowed back in the shop since!

"Let me help you find the butter dish, Auntie Susan," Tiger kindly offered.

Tiger knelt on the floor next to her aunt and carefully started to unpack another box. She took out an old, brown and white pin-striped jacket near the top of the box.

Underneath was a bundle of papers, which appeared at a glance to be some comics. However, just as Tiger was about to take these out of the box, her attention was drawn back to the jacket on the floor. Something silver was just showing at the top of one of the pockets.

"What's this?" Tiger asked her aunt as she pulled a silver pocket watch out of the jacket.

Mum looked surprised. "Gosh, this is from the Grey's house clearance last week," she said, as she took the watch off Tiger to study it a little more closely. "I remember putting the jacket in the box, but I did not see the watch. What a nice surprise. I can't see a hallmark or any manufacturer's details, so it may not be worth a great deal. However, it is a nice-looking watch. Pocket watches like this sell very quickly. I think I will put it in the shop just as soon as I have researched it," Mum explained to Tiger.

Tiger thought it a beautiful-looking watch and felt quite pleased with herself that she had found it. She wondered if the jacket would have been sold without her aunt ever having known about the watch. Some lucky customer would have had a wonderful surprise! Alternatively, what if her Auntie Susan had just sent the jacket off to recycling? The watch may never have been found!

"Please can I research it?" Tiger asked her aunt eagerly. "I can take it down to the library tomorrow morning. I know how to do it." Tiger was very studious and had often helped her aunt with valuations and research in the past.

"Yes, of course you can, Tiger. How helpful," Mum said ever so smugly, whilst throwing Red and Tank one of her 'why can't you be this helpful?' looks. "You can all go to the library for an hour. Then you can come to the shop with the watch and tell me all that you have found out about it. At least that way I will know what you are all up to tomorrow morning," Mum told the four of them.

Red was not annoyed with Tiger. He knew Mum was happy to find an excuse for the children not to spend a whole day on the Trail. Red often heard Mum promising Auntie Angela that the girls would not get hurt when on holiday. Mum always said there was less chance of that if the girls were not copying the boys on the Trail. No doubt because most school holidays involved a trip to the hospital for one of the boys.

Last holiday, Tank cut his leg when he fell out of a tree. He had needed five stitches. It had been really bad and Mum had to remind Tank of that fact when he was proudly showing off his stitches to his school friends on the following Monday.

Tank had also broken two fingers the holiday before when his bicycle went one way and he went the other. Tank had blamed it on a squirrel that had run out in front of him. Red had never told a soul, not even Tank, that he had seen Tank fall off whilst trying to ride no-handed. Red was so agile and strong he had perfected riding the Trail for at least a mile without touching the handlebars. Tank so wanted to do that too, just like his brother. Red had to push both bicycles four miles home that day and Tank had whined the entire time. Still, Red had kept quiet about what he had seen to save his little brother's embarrassment.

Red had not needed quite so many

hospital visits as Tank over the years, although Red's legs were just a mass of bruises and cuts merged together, leaving just a little pink skin here and there. Despite Mum's concerns, Tiger and Fudge had successfully avoided going home to Reading with any injuries to date. Mum was relieved when she could tell Auntie Angela at the end of the holiday that the girls were unharmed. However, Dad always said that Mum should just stop worrying and that whatever happened in life, including any wounds or injuries, was character building.

Tank, however, could not bear the thought of being stuck inside the library for an hour researching. He confidently told Mum that the four of them had already planned their day on the Trail tomorrow, so they wouldn't have time for the library. Had Tank not finished his sentence with his dimpled smile, Red is sure Mum would have told Tank off for being rude. Mum was not prepared to negotiate though, and she said her decision was final. Tank looked like he was going to erupt.

"Great, tomorrow is going to be the

worst day of my life!" said Tank angrily.

Everyone could not help but laugh at Tank. He was always so melodramatic. Tank knew he was too. Dad was often telling him he would make a fortune as an actor when he was older. Red laughed along too, but he also knew that his little brother needed consoling otherwise he would get upset.

"Come on, Tank, we can still have fun in the library and in town before we go on to the Trail," reassured Red. "We always have fun with the girls no matter what we do. Perhaps Mum will let us stay out longer on the Trail in the afternoon to thank us for helping her in the morning."

Mum was smiling at Red. He was such a kind and caring brother. "That's a deal kids," Mum replied. "And if your research on the watch is good, then I will let you each buy a quarter of sweets from Mr Jolley's."

The children were delighted, including Tank now, as Mr Jolley's was the most wonderful sweet shop the children had ever been to. The shop window was so eye-catching that even people rushing by would stop to admire the various sweets on display.

Different fudges, chocolates, sherbets, liquorices, marshmallows, nougats, jellies, lozenges, lollipops, toffees and any other sweet you could think of filled the large glass jars. If the window display was not able to tempt you in, then the delicious aroma that wafted in the air when the shop door was opened definitely would. Mr Jolley was a really funny man too and always nice to the children when they went into the shop.

It was getting late and the children were tired after their long bike ride. They all agreed that they would aim to be at the library for nine o'clock tomorrow morning. That way, they could perhaps be on the Trail by eleven o'clock. Mum offered to make them a delicious packed lunch, which the children could take to eat by the rope swing.

Red and Tank were in bed first. They were staying in Red's room and Tank was on a makeshift camp bed on the floor.

"Make sure you brush your teeth, boys!" Mum shouted up the stairs.

Neither boy replied. They were too

busy talking about what they would buy in Mr Jolley's. Tank's mouth was already watering at the thought of a quarter of his favourite toffee bon bons.

Tiger lay down on the inflatable mattress in Tank's room. She was admiring the watch she had found and could not wait to help Auntie Susan with the valuation. Tiger knew she could find some books in the library to help her with the task. She would need to find similar-looking watches, or perhaps she may be lucky and find a match – a photo and description of one exactly the same as this watch with its shiny, silver casing and large gold numbers. Tiger was sure the creamy, yellow-coloured face was faded or discoloured, perhaps due to the age of the watch. A long silver chain hung down from the ring on the top of the watch.

Tiger slid her fingers over the cold metal and wondered who this watch had belonged to. The back of the watch felt slightly bumpy and, on closer inspection, Tiger could see there were some words engraved on the metal.

"Fudge, listen to this," said Tiger. "The

watch has writing on the back. It says 'To my darling George, with much affection. Alice'. I wonder who George and Alice are. I wonder if we could find that out, Fudge."

Fudge did not answer. Tiger then heard a very faint snore from Tank's bed where Fudge was sleeping.

"Night, Fudge," Tiger whispered.

Tiger carefully placed the watch in her slipper beside the mattress. Tiger had a feeling this watch was special and she just could not wait to find out why.

Chapter 4

The tunnel revisited

"See you in the shop!" Red shouted to Mum as he shut the front door behind him. The children were well ahead of schedule. It was only twenty minutes past eight and they were already leaving for the library, which was not open for another forty minutes. Red was always up and out early anyway. The girls usually preferred to have a little lie-in, but not today. All four children had risen early and were now eagerly walking through the hamlet towards the little dirt track that led to the Trail. They had left their bicycles at home as they had decided to collect these with their packed lunch later, after their trip to Mr Jolley's.

As the children walked down the woodland track towards the Trail, they caught glimpses of Mr Jolley's bright pink walls through the trees, the shop beckoning them from afar.

"It's just like a giant strawberry bon bon," said Tank, now undecided whether to buy the strawberry or toffee bon bons. It was a hard decision, as they were both scrumptious.

"I just can't wait to get my bag of Mr Jolley's sweets," squealed Fudge.

All four children skipped down the hill, Tiger clutching the watch in her right pocket as she did so, just to make sure she did not lose it. Auntie Susan had reminded her to hold the watch tight all the way. This was one of the reasons why the children had decided to leave their bicycles at home for the morning. Auntie Susan had told Tiger that there was more chance of her losing or breaking the watch if she cycled into town.

The Trail was in sight. It was probably only about another fifty metres down the hill until the track they were on joined the Trail. Suddenly, Tank, who was leading the way, turned round and faced the girls. "Ha, ha, you missed it," he said, teasing the girls because they had walked right past the tunnel entrance.

"We weren't looking for it," replied Fudge defensively.

"Fudge is right. We aren't going down the tunnel so the girls weren't looking out for it, Tank," said Red protectively. Red put his hands on Fudge's shoulders and turned her around, pointing her in the direction of the tunnel entrance. "Just for the record, girls. See the oak tree there?" he said as he nodded his head towards the enormous tree at the side of the track nearby. "As soon as you are level with the trunk, you need to leave the track on the other side. Take about twelve large steps. Come on," urged Red as he encouraged Tiger and Fudge to follow him, counting out the steps together as they did so.

Before the children had even counted to five, Tank had managed to brush past them to get ahead, desperately trying to be the first one there. Tank did not even flinch when he was caught on a prickly bush *en route*. With a quick tug of his shorts, he was soon freed from the thorny trap.

"Tank, you have just made a hole in your shorts," Tiger pointed out.

"Hey presto!" announced Tank, whilst pointing to the tunnel entrance, as if he had just performed a magic trick, and not at all worried about the tear in his shorts.

This tunnel opening did not look quite as scary as the one down by the river bank. This access was not covered by ivy and bushes, so it appeared much lighter inside the tunnel. Red and Tank had not thought it necessary to camouflage this entrance, as not many people walked along the track from the hamlet to the Trail and it was not physically possible to see the tunnel from the track in any event. Besides, covering it up would have made the tunnel too dark to venture down without a torch or bicycle lights, and Red and Tank did not always have their bicycles with them.

In a flash, Fudge had run into the tunnel. "Wheeeeeeeee!" she shouted as she ran at speed through the tunnel, her cry getting fainter and fainter as she disappeared out of sight.

Tiger was concerned. They were on a tight time schedule to get to the library and she did not share Fudge's enthusiasm for going back in the tunnel today. Tiger had found the tunnel a little scary yesterday. Also, she did not want to get her best holiday outfit dirty. Tiger had put on her favourite jean dungarees to go into town, as she had planned to change into her older clothes before they cycled to the bird hide later.

"We haven't got time for this, Fudge!" yelled Tiger as she poked her head into the tunnel. "It is nearly half past eight! We need to get to the library! If you come back now, we can play in here later!"

Red, Tank and Tiger looked at each other waiting for Fudge to respond or, better still, appear back at the entrance. But nothing, not a sound.

"Come on," said Red. "We are early, anyway. We might as well go this way now. It will only add a few minutes on to the journey."

Tiger was not at all keen but, anxious to check her little sister was all right, she followed Red and Tank into the tunnel. The three quickly made their way down. Tank stopped for a moment to pick up a stick, which he then used to rhythmically tap against the inside of the tunnel wall as he ran after Red. There was no sound from Fudge, despite Tiger calling out to her a few more times. Red stopped and turned around to reassure Tiger that they were nearly approaching the end of the tunnel when all three children were taken by complete surprise.

"Boo!" screamed Fudge, whilst jumping up from her crouched position and squealing with delight that she had tricked them. "Made you jump."

Even Red and Tank had jumped a mile, although Tank insisted he had not and that he had spotted Fudge well before she booed them. Tiger was quick to tell Fudge off, "Don't run off again! We were worried about you."

Fudge apologised and gave Tiger an exaggerated bear hug to show just how sorry she was.

"It's all right, Fudge, just don't do it again," pleaded Tiger, whilst gently removing Fudge's dirty hands from her clean dungarees.

"Right, everybody, out and to the library," ordered Red as he led the way out of the tunnel entrance, pushing aside the trailing ivy as he did so.

———◦◦◦———

As the children came out of the tunnel they were all a little dazzled by the early morning sun, their eyes taking a while to adjust after having been in the dimly-lit tunnel. Tank rubbed his eyes and, as he lowered his hands, he could not quite believe what he saw. Well, what he did *not* see to be exact. He rubbed his eyes again before taking a long, hard look at the brow of the hill.

"No way! It can't be. Where has Tanner's Farm gone?" he asked. "Look, look at the hill everyone. The farmhouse is not there. Red, where has it gone?"

Before Red had a chance to reply, all of them were startled by a horrendous clanking noise followed by a tremendous thud from behind them. It was so deafeningly loud and unexpected that all four children dropped to the ground to take cover, not at all sure what it was.

"What was that?" asked Red.

Red and Tank were lying still on the

ground, trying to work out what could possibly have made the eerie clanking and crashing noise. Fudge was the first who dared to stand up and started to brush away a few leaves and mud from her clothes. Her hands were still a little dusty too from where she had crouched in the tunnel, so she was actually making her outfit a little dirtier with each wipe she made.

"Wow, look at your clothes," said Tank to Fudge. "They are different to what you were wearing before."

Fudge held the bottom of her outfit and as she looked down she could not quite believe it. Her clothes were, as Tank said, completely different. Her dress was no longer the pretty pink cotton material with white spots. It was now a thick cotton pinafore and a very dull brown colour.

"My pretty outfit. It's gone. What's happened to my clothes and why am I wearing this?" she asked, as she looked distastefully down at her new outfit and tugged the collar of the white cotton blouse she was now wearing underneath the pinafore.

"It's not just *your* clothes," said Red, now standing up with his arms spread out wide as he looked down at his new attire. "Look at us. Our clothes have changed too."

Red's favourite blue T-shirt had gone and he was now wearing a cream flannel shirt. His ripped denim shorts had been replaced by a smarter pair of brown shorts. Tank's outfit was very similar to Red's, although he was also now wearing a floppy woollen cap instead of the baseball cap he had been sporting earlier. His shorts were also being held up by a pair of brown braces.

"What are these?" said Tank, as he comically stretched the braces as far as they could go in front of him.

"Great braces, Tank," said Fudge, nudging him in the elbow. "You do look funny."

"Tiger. Where's Tiger?" Red quickly interrupted, realising that she was not with them. Red looked around and saw Tiger much further down the bank on her hands and knees. "What are you doing Tiger, are you OK?" he shouted down to her.

"I've lost it!" Tiger shouted back. "I can't

find the watch. I think I must have dropped it when that noise scared us. It must have fallen down the bank as I had it when we were in the tunnel. Please help me find it, Red, or Auntie Susan will be cross. I promised her I would keep it safe."

Red could see how worried Tiger was. She was frantically searching on her hands and knees on the steep and dirty bank. Red told Tank and Fudge to stay where they were, just outside the tunnel entrance, whilst he went down to help Tiger. Red thought the bank was far too steep and slippery for the younger ones.

"It's not here," said Red after a couple of minutes of scouring the bank with Tiger. "We would definitely see it if it was here. Are you sure you dropped it, Tiger?"

Tiger was not at all sure what had happened. "I just don't know," she replied. "That horrific noise just frightened me so much that when I dropped down I somehow stumbled even further down the bank. I can only think that the watch fell out of my pocket as I fell."

"Well, it isn't here," said Red impatiently

and, as he turned around, he could see that neither Fudge nor Tank were waiting by the tunnel entrance as he had asked them to. Red sighed. "Why did I think they would listen to me?" he said, as he saw the two of them making their way up towards the Trail.

"Come on, Tiger, we can come back and look for the watch later," said Red as he started running up the bank towards the Trail. "It won't have gone far. Something far more important is going on. Take a look at your clothes, Tiger. All of our outfits have changed and Tanner's Farm has vanished. Now Tank and Fudge are nearly out of sight. We'd best hurry and catch up with them as something really, really strange is happening."

Tiger looked down at her dungarees. They were no longer the pretty and stylish jean dungarees she had put on earlier that morning, but rather plain dungarees in a mushroom-coloured material that Tiger would definitely not choose to wear. Tiger was worried about the watch, but Red was right, the search for it could wait. She did not wish to be left alone, so she hurried up the bank to catch up with Red.

As Red neared the top of the bank, he was glad to see Tank and Fudge waiting for them.

"Hurry, Red, this is amazing!" Tank shouted to Red.

As Red reached the top, he simply gasped. Red stood there open-mouthed and speechless. There, where the Trail should have been, where they played and cycled every day, was now a long expanse of railway track, stretching as far as the eye could see in both directions.

Tiger, too, soon appeared at the top of the bank. She was very red in the face and out of breath for having run up the bank so fast. "A railway line, but how?" was all she managed to say before leaning against a large white post at the side of the track to catch her breath.

"That's it," said Red, pointing to the signal at the top of the post. "That must be what made that loud noise. The signal must have changed and when it did that big metal weight must have clonked against the post. I reckon that is what caused the noise."

"Listen," said Fudge. "I can hear

something coming."

They all stopped and listened. Fudge was right. There was a faint sound coming from the Wadebridge direction. It was hard to make out what the noise was at first, until Fudge cried out, "I think it's a train!"

"Oh, yes, I hope so," added Tank.

Red told them all to be quiet and listen some more so they could be sure. Sure enough, a train was coming. They could now hear the distant sound of the wheels on the track.

"It's getting nearer. Here it comes!" Tiger shouted, pointing to the train making its way through the trees in the distance.

A 'Toot Toot' blasted out from the train. "Do you think it is tooting us?" asked Fudge.

"The driver won't have seen us yet, so probably not," said Red.

"I don't know, it is actually coming towards us terribly fast!" screamed Tiger.

"Everyone to the side of the track," ordered Red.

The children quickly got off the track but, somehow, in the mad rush, Tank and Tiger had jumped to one side of the track and Red and Fudge to the other.

"Stay where you are and get down!" Red shouted to Tank and Tiger, worried in case either of them tried to join him and Fudge on the other side of the track. Red felt much better when he saw Tiger firmly take Tank's hand as they crouched down near the bushes on the verge opposite.

Red lay on the floor next to Fudge and he protectively put his arm around her. Fudge did not seem as though she needed comforting, but Red felt reassured to know that she was not going anywhere until the train had passed.

"Wow, it's a lovely steam train, just like the one we went on yesterday," said Fudge as the beautiful engine came rushing towards them.

Within seconds, the train reached the spot where the children lay. The children watched intently as the train loudly clunked over the metal tracks right before their very eyes. It passed ever so quickly, but as each of the six carriages passed by Red took a quick look through to the other side of the verge. He could just make out Tiger and Tank still safely huddled next to each other on the ground, their eyes fixed on the passing train.

As the final carriage passed by, the children heard a screeching sound.

"It's braking, it's actually going to stop!" shouted Tank. "Do you think they saw us?"

The four of them got to their feet and hurried on to the track. They could see the back of the train quite a way in the distance and they watched as the train slowly grinded to a halt. Red could just about make out a very small platform in a cutting in between the trees. The children did not see any passengers get on or off the train. They heard a faint whistle before the train pulled away. It slowly chugged its way around the corner leaving beautiful, white clouds of smoke gracefully drifting in the sky above.

"That was close, wasn't it?" said Fudge.

"What is going on?" asked Tiger, looking at Red for an answer.

Red was trying to make sense of it all, although it just didn't make any sense.

"We know that train was an actual steam engine and we are standing on a real railway track," said Red, pausing to think before he started again. "There was a railway line here on the Trail years ago that ran from Wadebridge to Wenfordbridge and Bodmin. I am sure I have read somewhere that the passenger trains used to run until 1967."

Red started pacing up and down the track before continuing. "Then there is the mystery of Tanner's Farm disappearing. I remember Dad telling me that he was about ten when the farmhouse was built, so that means it was probably built in 1965. So we have steam trains and no Tanner's Farm. The only explanation must be...," Red paused. "But it can't be. How could it be?"

"Tell us, tell us," begged Fudge impatiently.

"We must have gone back in time to, well, to sometime before 1965," Red found himself saying, actually not quite believing it himself. "That would explain why we are in these clothes, too, I think."

"Gone back in time!" exclaimed Tank.

"But how?" asked Fudge.

"This can't be real, can it?" asked Tiger.

They were questions none of them could answer. As they watched the trail of smoke slowly fade away above the now deserted railway line, the four of them realised this was already the strangest adventure they had ever had!

Chapter 5

Lancelot, again

The children had all pinched themselves long and hard enough to know that this was not a dream. They had gone back in time, but how had they got here, why were they here and exactly what year was it?

Red was not afraid. He felt strangely confident, convinced there was a reason why they were on this adventure and he and Fudge were eager to explore. Tank so wanted to see another steam train, but he was also a little reluctant to wander off too far. Tank was surprised at Fudge's enthusiasm to go with Red and he did not wish to show any sign of weakness. Tank, therefore, put on a brave face and said he was ready to venture further along the track.

Tiger would have been happy going straight back to find the watch, and then trying to get home. However, Tiger knew that she was going to have to explore with the others whether she liked it or not. She could tell there was no way she would be able to convince them all to turn around now.

Red could see Tiger was concerned. He so hated her to be upset. "It will be all right," he discretely whispered in her ear, not wishing to embarrass her in front of Tank and Fudge.

Red promised Tiger that they would turn straight back if there was any sign of trouble.

Tiger respected Red's courage and strength of character. She knew he would do whatever he could to protect them and she trusted him. Besides, there was no way Tiger was going back up the tunnel alone. They agreed that they would not stray from the track and only venture a little further along, perhaps to their favourite rope swing spot.

The children soon reached the platform that the steam train had just pulled away from. It was a very small platform without any ticket office or shelter. On a white picket fence there was a wooden sign, painted green with pretty gold lettering which read 'The Shooting Range'. In the middle of the fence there was a gate, which opened on to a windy, narrow track.

"I wonder where that little path leads," said Fudge.

Red was not sure at all. "I don't know about the path, but that sign is familiar," he said. "The Shooting Range sign is the same sign as the one we see on the Trail, where we ride our bikes up the small bank."

"Oh, yes, I know where you mean," said Tank. "Is the bank we cycle up actually this platform?"

"I reckon so," said Red, as he and Tank ran up and down the platform.

"You know what that means, don't you?" said Tank, stopping abruptly in front of Red. "Mad Meeks' cottage is just around the corner. I wonder if he is there."

"If he is and we have gone back in time, then he won't be a grumpy old man, will he?" joked Red. "Come on, let's just go a little further. We can go past Mad Meeks' cottage and then on to Grogley Halt. We can see if there is another station there."

It was ever so quiet. There was simply no one else about and even Tiger felt safe. The children went just a little further until they could see River View Cottage in the distance.

"It looks just the same. Come on, race you there for a game of pooh sticks!" shouted Tank as he raced off towards the cottage, doing a strange little jig as he quickly stepped in and out of the railway tracks.

Fudge set off after Tank, copying his moves as she did so. "Wait for me, Tank!" she shouted, stumbling a little as she followed.

"Be careful, Fudge!" Tiger shouted ahead, worried that her little sister was going to fall over and hurt herself.

Red insisted that he and Tiger catch up with Tank and Fudge, just in case a train was to come along. Red could not hear one in the distance, but he thought it far safer that they all stayed as close together as possible.

After the last train had passed, Red had told them all how vigilant they must be and they had actually rehearsed what they would do if another train came along. At the first sight or sound of a train, Red had instructed them to all go to the right of the track, and not separate sides as they had done before. Then, to take at least five strides into the woodland before taking cover. That way, they would be a safe distance away from any passing train.

Tank had comically acted out flagging down a train, falling down on the track and the train then only just stopping inches before him. Red had told Tank he was silly, as it was only in films that trains stopped like that in the nick of time. Red told Tank that they must stay safe and that trying to stop a train was going to bring unnecessary attention to themselves.

Tiger had burst out laughing, not at Tank's acting abilities but at the topic of conversation. "I can't believe we are actually talking about flagging down a steam train, and what on earth would Mummy say if she knew that we were walking on a real railway line?" she said. Everyone laughed as Tiger was right.

"There it is, Mad Meeks' cottage!" Fudge cried out as she and Tank ran off the track and towards it. Tiger caught up with Fudge and they both ran to the back garden wall. Tiger was able to admire the colourful display of flowers and plants in the back garden, as she was just tall enough to peer over the wall. "Wow! It's as beautiful as ever," she told Fudge.

"I can't see," said Fudge angrily. Even on the tips of her toes she was just a little bit too small to see over the wall. Fudge was just a little too heavy for Tiger to lift up and Red was not there to help. He and Tank had already run to the front of the cottage and were in the middle of a game of pooh sticks when the girls caught up with them.

"I want to play too," squealed Fudge as she picked up a stick and threw it in the water.

Tiger did not join in or watch the others play. Instead, she carefully studied the cottage, just to be sure there was no one watching them. Tiger had not seen anybody in the garden and there was no sign of anyone at the windows. Somehow, today, the cottage did not seem quite as scary. In fact, it looked ever so pretty. The window frames appeared freshly painted and the front garden looked ever so different too. The garden had a border either side of the cobbled path, which led to the front door. Both borders were filled with stunning, red and pink flowers soaking up the morning sun.

"Any sign of him?" Tank called over to Tiger.

"I don't think he lives here," said Tiger. "The cottage looks different. For a start, the front garden has lots of flowers. Mad Meeks does not bother with his front garden. Oh, yes, and look over there too," said Tiger, pointing to the side of the bank.

Red, Tank and Fudge turned to look.

"What? What is it?" asked Tank, with a puzzled look on his face. "I can't see what you are looking at."

"That's exactly it," replied Tiger. "There's nothing there. Those scary warning signs outside Mad Meeks' aren't here." Tiger now felt herself relaxing far more than she had before. There really was nothing to worry about she thought.

Tiger joined in the pooh sticks competition. Somehow, Tank managed to win every one of the next five races. He assured the others it was just good luck, but the girls were certain he did something special to his sticks to make them go faster, although they were not at all sure what it could be. Fudge proposed one more game but Red said no, as he was keen to follow the railway line a little further to Grogley Halt. They agreed that they would perhaps have another couple of races on the way back.

Red led the way rather briskly along the track, only stopping now and again to see if they could actually spot the woodpecker that they had heard pecking away for the last five minutes.

"Did you know it is called yaffing?" Red told the others. "Yaffing is the technical name for the sound a woodpecker makes when it pecks at the tree."

Red was full of interesting facts about the wildlife on the Trail and he always took great pleasure in sharing what he knew with the girls.

When the boys were younger, Mum and Dad had gone up and down the Trail telling them all about the different species of trees, animals and insects they saw. Red had absorbed it all, sometimes asking questions that Mum and Dad did not know the answer to. Mum often said Red had a real appetite for facts and was just like Dad for retaining them. "A brain like a sponge," Mum would say, although she never understood how Red remembered all the scientific names and facts he was taught yet somehow could never remember the time he was meant to be home for tea!

⚬⚬⚬

After quite a walk, the children could see a break in the trees a little further down the track and what looked like a large block of concrete next to it.

"There it is. That will be Grogley Halt station," said Red confidently. "Doesn't look like there is anyone about again. Come on, let's go and take a look," he said as he beckoned the others to keep following him.

The four of them left the track and ran up the concrete ramp towards the station. There was a little shelter, big enough to house perhaps six to eight people from bad weather. Next to it was a large wooden sign displaying the station name.

"You're right, Red. It is Grogley Halt," said Fudge as she trailed her finger across the shiny painted sign.

The children realised that they had got to this station without spotting their rope swing hideout. Everything looked different now there was no Trail.

They spent a little while looking around this station, but there was very little to see. Again, there was no ticket office here, so the children wondered whether the trains actually stopped here.

As the children were standing right on the edge of the platform, they all imagined what it would be like if a train was coming. Tank pretended to be the Guard and Fudge the Ticket Collector. Red and Tiger walked arm in arm, taking on the roles of an incredibly important Lord and Lady.

"Take our bags please, Guard," Red said ever so poshly. Tank hurried along and picked up the imaginary cases. Fudge pretended to stamp their tickets.

"First class at the front of the train, my Lord and Lady," said Fudge, whilst performing an exaggerated curtsy.

"Don't curtsy," Red scolded Fudge mockingly. "You are a male Guard. Bow, you fool."

Although they had been having great fun, Tiger told the others she thought they should be heading back now. The others agreed that they could be ages waiting to see if a train came and they were all quite keen for a game of pooh sticks on the way back anyway.

As the children were about to leave, they heard a noise in the distance.

"I think it's a train," said Fudge.

"It does sound like it," said Red, as the familiar huffing and puffing of the engine could be heard.

"There it is, see the smoke!" Tiger shouted out, pointing to the train making its way through the trees in the distance.

"It's Lancelot," said Fudge. "Look, Red, I'm sure it is."

Sure enough, the bright red and green engine chugged its way to the platform and proudly stopped just where the children were standing. The Guard stepped on to the platform at the rear of the train. He waved to the children, as if gesturing for them to board the train.

"We can't get on, we don't have any tickets," said Tank.

"But the driver has stopped for us," said Fudge.

Red thought about it. "Well, we actually only need to travel one stop to The Shooting Range," he said. "It is such a short distance away so we will be there in no time at all. There probably won't be any time for the Ticket Collector to check the tickets. I reckon we should sit in the first carriage too. If the Guard at the back of the train is the one who checks the tickets, he probably won't even have time to walk to the first carriage."

"Come on then everyone," said Tank, running to the door of the first carriage.

Before Red and Tiger knew it, Tank and Fudge were already seated in the first carriage. There were other people in there too.

"We can't make a scene now," said Tiger.

"Come on then, what have we got to lose?" Red said, gently taking Tiger's hand as he helped her up on to the train.

Red and Tiger took the two seats opposite Tank and Fudge. There were three other people on the other side of the carriage, but none of them paid any particular attention to Red and Tiger as they sat down. The final seat in their carriage was quickly filled by a very smartly-dressed boy, just before the loud blow of the whistle marked the train's departure.

Red breathed a sigh of relief as the train slowly pulled out of the station. Not long, he thought, until they were at The Shooting Range and he would insist that they make their way home then.

Red closed his eyes for a second. Was this a dream? he wondered. What had actually happened and just how would he get them all safely home?

Tiger gasped and then elbowed Red in the ribs. Red quickly opened his eyes to see a very strict-looking Guard standing directly in front of him.

"Your tickets please…"

Chapter 6

Theft on the train

Red felt the perspiration on his brow. He wondered how he could have let them get into this situation. The train was moving, so there was no escape now. He was somehow going to have to explain that they had no tickets, and no money to buy any. Red hoped that none of the others tried to explain why. If anyone was to mention that they had travelled back in time from 1995, that would be sure to get them all locked up! The Guard would think they were all mad, or worse than that, perhaps he would think they were criminals trying to avoid paying their fares. Red knew he had to think of something, and quick.

"Tickets, young man," said the Guard sternly.

"I…, well, you see, I…," Red stuttered, desperately trying to find the right words to say.

"Red," said Fudge.

"Not now, Fudge. Let me deal with this please," said Red, glaring at his cousin to stop her getting involved.

Fudge ignored Red. She reached into the pocket in her pinafore dress and pulled out her purse. She opened the little side pocket and pulled out the four tickets the Ticket Collector had given her yesterday, when they were on Lancelot. Fudge tapped the Guard on his arm and, as he turned around to look at her, she confidently held out the four, unpunched tickets.

"But those tickets are…," said Red.

"Those tickets are for the four of us," interrupted Fudge, as she gave the Guard a wonderfully angelic smile.

The Guard took the four tickets off Fudge and held them just under his nose as he carefully inspected each one.

Red mopped the large droplets of sweat from his brow with the top of his shirt sleeve. It seemed like the Guard was taking ages to look at them. He wondered what trouble his little cousin was going to get them into. He was sure that being accused of forging tickets was far worse than simply having no tickets at all. Perhaps he should have told the Guard right at the start that they had lost their tickets, but he had just not been able to think quickly enough.

The Guard bent down towards Fudge and stared straight at her. Tiger gasped.

"Well, thank you, little Miss," the Guard then said with a beaming smile. He neatly punched a hole in the corner of each ticket before handing them back to Fudge.

Both Red and Tiger breathed a sigh of relief as the Guard turned to speak to the young male who had joined their carriage after them.

"Phew," said Tank.

Red put his index finger over his mouth, urging all of them to now keep quiet. Red then simply leant forward and quickly whispered to Fudge, "Well done. Proud of you, Fudge."

They had not travelled much further when Tiger nudged Red. "Look at that lady," said Tiger quietly.

Red followed Tiger's line of vision and saw the lady sitting on the other side of the carriage.

"What about her?" Red whispered back, not at all sure why Tiger had pointed her out.

"Her outfit, silly," said Tiger. "She looks just like a film star – like the ones in the black and white war films."

The lady was probably about thirty five or so, thought Tiger. Her hair was meticulously pulled back into a neat bun and she was wearing a small brown hat, elegantly tilted to one side of her head. A fluffy brown and white feather on the rim of the hat bounced up and down with the movement of the train. A tweed cape lined with a cream silky material rested effortlessly over her shoulders. Underneath, she wore a cream and brown dress, a gold belt drawing in the material at her very tiny waist. She was holding a pair of brown leather gloves with one hand; the other beautifully manicured hand was resting gently on her leg. Tiger just could not take her eyes off her.

The lady was looking lovingly at a handsome gentleman sitting opposite her. His brown trilby hat and brown and white pin-striped suit matched her outfit perfectly.

"What time is it please, George?" asked the lady.

The gentleman looked down at his suit. He pulled open his jacket and then slipped his right hand into the chest pocket of his matching waistcoat. He pulled something out and, as he opened his hand, Tiger could see it was a silver chain with a silver watch attached.

"Well, I say, Alice, it is nearly ten o'clock," he replied in a posh voice.

"Wonderful, George. We must be nearly there," replied the lady.

Tiger was still staring at the watch as the gentleman carefully placed it back inside his waistcoat pocket.

"Tiger, stop staring," said Red. "Are you all right, Tiger? You look as if you have seen a ghost."

"Red, did you see?" Tiger said, a little too excitedly as she started jumping up and down in her seat. "The watch! That man, he has our pocket watch."

"Sshhh, Tiger," said Red. "What do you mean he has our watch?"

Tiger calmed down a little and quietly explained to Red that the gentleman was wearing exactly the same pocket watch that Tiger had lost.

"It has to be the same one," she said. "They called each other George and Alice. The writing on the back of the watch, it read from Alice to George. I am sure of it. Please, Red, that's our watch, we have to get it back."

Red could see part of the silver chain sticking out of the gentleman's waistcoat, but he could not see the actual watch.

"What are you thinking, Red?" asked Tiger. "What shall we do?"

Red was not sure at all. He did not know what he could do or say as it was obviously the gentleman's watch. There were other people travelling in the carriage too.

There was the very smartly-dressed boy who had joined their carriage just after them. Red had thought it a little strange at the time, as the boy had not been waiting on the platform with them. He had quite literally appeared from nowhere. He was dressed in a smart jacket and trousers with a crisp white shirt. Red was not at all sure how old he was.

He was perhaps only about fifteen, but he was dressed so smartly he looked as if he was on his way to work. His hair was neatly parted and gelled down.

Red could not see who the other passenger was. He had been reading a large newspaper when the children got on the train and had not put it down once. The newspaper completely covered the passenger's face, so all Red could see were dark trousers and a pair of very muddy lace-up boots.

"Red!" Tiger whispered impatiently, keen for Red to tell her what his plan was.

"Look at the paper," he replied. Red shifted forward so he was on the edge of his seat.

Tiger leant in closer to Red. "Can you see what date is on the newspaper?"

Red could not see that far. The writing was too small. Red and Tiger both squinted, trying to work out the small type on the paper. It was no good. The newspaper was just that little bit too far away.

"We're slowing down," said Tank, jumping up from his seat to get a better view of the nearing platform. Tank seemed completely carefree and not at all worried about drawing attention to himself.

"Sit down, Tank, and please keep your voice down a little," urged Red. "We will get off here though. It will be The Shooting Range station."

Tiger nudged Red. "What about the watch though?"

"There is nothing we can do," replied Red, as he glanced over at the silver chain dangling down from the man's pocket. "We just have to get off and find our way back. It's not our watch really, is it?"

As the train grinded to a very noisy halt, Red gave the nod for all of the children to follow him. Red confidently stood up and stepped into the aisle to lead the others off the train.

The smartly-dressed boy had also stood up rather quickly and he pushed his way past Red to get to the carriage door first. Red thought it rather strange that a boy dressed like a young gentleman had such bad manners. Red did not say anything though. He thought it best to keep quiet.

Red watched as the boy leant out of the train window and opened the train door before jumping out. Red was intrigued by the back of the boy's head. There was not a hair out of place as it appeared to be flattened down with some sort of wet gel. Red wondered if it was 'Brylcreem™' that Dad had once talked about using when he was younger. Red laughed to himself thinking that he would need a tub of cream each day if he was to tame his wild curls.

As Red stepped down from the train, he turned around to ensure the others were still with him. Tank and Fudge jumped on to the platform, followed by Tiger who stepped down ever so gracefully. Red then politely held the door open for the final passenger who was getting off.

All Red saw at first was the pair of muddy boots descending down the steps. He guessed it was the man who had been sitting holding the paper. Red looked up and studied the man. He looked about the same age as Dad, about forty, as he had the same silver grey streaks in his hair. He had a wonderfully tanned complexion and a very kind and jolly face.

Red thought he seemed familiar. He was sure he had seen him somewhere before, but he could not think where.

"Thank you, young man," said the man, smiling and bowing his head at Red as he reached the bottom step. The newspaper was tucked under the man's arm. As he walked past, Red tried to see the date on the paper. Yet, it was folded in such a way that Red could not see the date. Red felt helpless as he watched the man close the station gate behind him and take the path into the woods.

"Come on," said Red. "Let's get out of here too. That path should take us home."

———❦———

The four of them were only a little way down the path when they heard a commotion behind them. The children stopped and turned around to see what was going on. They could just about see over the station fence.

They saw George, the gentleman with the lady, leaning out of the door of the carriage and looking up and down the platform.

"Thief! There's a thief about!" he shouted towards the Guard, who was standing further down the platform. "Someone has stolen my watch!"

Tiger turned to Red. "Please tell me you haven't taken the watch," she said. "We are so in trouble now."

"Of course I haven't taken it," replied Red. "I can't believe you actually think I could have stolen something."

"Well, I did say we needed to get it back," said Tiger. "I thought you had jolly well gone and done it."

The gentleman had jumped on to the platform now and was talking with the Guard. Suddenly, the Guard and the gentleman started making their way towards the station gate, which led on to the path where the children were standing.

Without wasting another moment, the four children ran away as quickly as they could. After just a short sprint, they could see the man with the newspaper under his arm just a little further down the path.

"Quick, we must climb down the bank now or we will get caught," ordered Red, as he hurried into the wooded bank at the side of the path. Red told the others to follow him so they could take cover a little further along the bank. Red had spotted a place where they could hide.

The children ran as fast as they could darting between the trees and bushes. The bank was steep and incredibly slippery in places. Fudge had lost her footing twice. Tank, who was very bravely bringing up the rear, grabbed Fudge the second time she fell, stopping her from sliding right down to the water's edge.

"You can do it, Fudge," said Tank, as he helped pull her further up the bank. Tank could see the tears in her eyes. It was unlike Fudge and, despite the friendly competiveness between them, he really did not like to see her upset. Tank was scared too. However, once Fudge had got back on her feet, he put his hand in the small of her back and guided her as quickly as he could along the steepest part of the bank. Red and Tiger were just a few feet away hiding in the bushes and just beyond them was Mad Meeks' cottage. Funnily, the sight of Mad Meeks' cottage actually made Tank feel much better, as he knew they were not far from home now, even if they were in a different year.

"Lie down and be quiet!" ordered Red as he threw himself to the ground and lay flat on his stomach.

As Red lay motionless, his face resting on the damp, spongy moss of the river bank, he contemplated what their next move should be. They could either lie in wait until the coast was absolutely clear or they could travel further along the river bank. Red had heard Fudge yelp each time she had slipped, so perhaps staying where they were was the safest option. He could just about hear one of the others breathing heavily and the birds tweeting in the trees above as he lay there. The good news was that he could not hear anybody coming after them.

Suddenly, there was an almighty splash in the water below them and then a cry for help.

"Help! Help me…,"

Red went stone cold. "No, oh no!" he wailed as he turned around to see which one of them had fallen into the water below…

Chapter 7

The rescue

Red stared at the swirling water below. He saw someone, their arms frantically waving above their head as they bobbed up and down in the river. Red could not see clearly who it was and, in an instant, the body was swept away further downstream. Red tried to keep the person within his sight, but the dense branches overhanging the river bank now obscured his view.

Red turned to the others. As he did so, he felt an overwhelming sense of relief to see Tiger, Tank and Fudge still next to him, safe on the bank. His heart was beating incredibly fast though. He did not know who he had seen struggling in the water but, whoever it was, he had to help them. There was simply no time to waste.

Red told Tiger and Fudge to stay where there were, out of sight just in case the gentleman and the Guard were still on their way down the path. Red urged them to hold on to the tree roots or branches as tightly as they could, so that they did not slide down the bank too.

Red directed Tank to follow him, so they could both help to rescue the person in the water.

They both hurried along the bank. They had perhaps only ventured about twenty metres or so when Red suddenly dropped down on to his knees, tugging at Tank's arm as he did so.

"Hey," said Tank, as he fell rather awkwardly.

Red immediately turned to Tank and put his index finger against his lips, urging Tank to remain quiet. Red stared long and hard at Tank. Tank knew not to say anything at all, even though he really wanted to shout at Red and tell him that his leg was hurting from the fall.

Tank glanced down and saw blood trickling down his left leg. He had fallen heavily on to a stone, which had caused quite a large gash near his knee cap.

Tank did not mind the sight of blood.

He had certainly seen a lot of it from all of the injuries he had sustained, usually on the Trail or the rugby pitch. Dad had told the boys that cuts sometimes looked far worse than they actually were, and it was often the case that more serious cuts were the ones when there was very little blood.

"It's really stinging," Tank whispered to Red.

Red looked over at Tank's leg. It was only a small wound in comparison to Tank's usual cuts and scrapes. Tank tried to fight the tears, but Red could see his eyes welling up. Tank rarely cried. He was usually such a brave boy with an unbelievably high pain threshold. Red so wanted to hug and comfort his brother but he just could not. If Red moved, he feared he would blow their cover and now was certainly not the time to do that! All Red could do was discretely squeeze his brother's hand as they both watched the man who had been on the train with the newspaper stagger up the slippery bank.

It seemed difficult for the man to keep his footing on the wet and muddy bank, as he was struggling with the weight of the lifeless body that lay draped across his arms. The man had a pained expression on his face and it seemed like he was quietly sobbing.

"Look, it's that newspaper man and he has saved that boy, the one from our carriage," said Tank. "He's not moving. Do you think he is…?"

"Ssshh now or they will hear us," interrupted Red. "Just wait."

Red and Tank waited silently. They watched as the man gently laid the boy on the path on his side. The boy spluttered a little before coughing up quite a lot of water.

Red exhaled loudly, a little too loudly for his own liking, so he put his hand over his mouth, worried in case the man heard him. Red was relieved that the man did not look over, but instead carried on tending to the boy.

He had sat the boy up now and was helping to remove his sopping wet jacket. His crisp white shirt was sodden and he was missing a shoe. The previously smart-looking boy now looked very weak and dishevelled.

"Let's go inside and get you warm, Richard, before you catch your death with cold," said the man to the boy. You can tell me what happened, how you came to be in the water. I will contact Henley Manor."

"Please don't," pleaded the boy. "Please don't."

"Nonsense," said the man as he helped the boy to his feet.

Suddenly, Red and Tank heard other voices further down the path. "They can't have got far!" they heard a male voice shout.

Almost immediately, the boy scooped up his jacket from the ground and ran further into the woodland on the other side of the track.

As the boy ran off, the children saw the man bend down and pick up something off the path. He looked at it and then shouted out after the boy. "Richard! Where are you going? Come back!"

The boy did not stop or turn around. He ran even faster and was out of sight within seconds.

"Thief!" shouted the Guard, as he and the gentleman approached the man. The pocket watch was in clear view as it rested in the man's open palm.

"You are nothing but a disgraceful

thief," said the gentleman. "Give me back my watch."

"Your watch?" said the man.

"Have you no shame?" replied the gentleman. "To steal it from me, from right under my very nose, and to then pretend nothing of it. There is no mistaking it is my watch. Henry Priddy, in Truro, designed and made only ten of these. He will vouch that Alice purchased it for me. Besides, the inscription on the back is proof enough."

The man turned the watch over and studied the writing on the back.

"Look at the state of you too," said the gentleman, shaking his head. "Why, you are drenched to the bone! I hope for your sake that my precious watch is not water damaged."

"Forgive me," replied the man. "I did not mean to be rude. I am afraid the watch may have been in the river. I do hope it is not damaged though."

"You are talking in riddles," said the gentleman crossly. "You pretend to be polite and apologetic, however, you are nothing more than a common criminal. Save your explanations for the police."

The Guard stepped forward and held out his hand. "Will you come quietly and allow us to conduct a citizen's arrest?"

"But you don't understand, I didn't...," said the man, abruptly stopping in mid-sentence.

"You didn't what?" asked the Guard.

The man paused. He did not answer. He looked down at the watch and then held out his hand in front of him. "I am very sorry," he said. "Please take it back and, yes, I will come. You will not have any trouble from me. I assure you of that."

"Very well. Come with us then and I will see that the police know that you have co-operated regarding the return of my watch," replied the gentleman.

Red and Tank were relieved to see the three men start walking along the path towards the station. When Red was sure they were out of earshot, he helped Tank to his feet.

"Sorry about your leg, Tank," Red said.

Tank had been concentrating so much on keeping hidden that he had actually forgotten about his wound. He looked down and could see the blood trickling a little further down his leg. Red did not have time to inspect it though, he was far more worried about the girls.

"I hope the girls are still hiding," said Red. "We need to get them and then get out of here as fast as we can."

"Wait a moment," said Tank as he started sliding down the bank a little.

"Stop! What are you doing?" asked Red. "Be careful, it's really dangerous."

Tank did not answer, but ventured just a little further down the bank. Red was curious as Tank grabbed hold of an overhanging branch with his left hand and then bent down, stretching as far as he could to pick up a newspaper lying in the mud.

"I wanted this," said Tank, as he dangled precariously from the branch and waved the newspaper in the air. "I bet it is that man's. You know, the one he was reading on the train. He must have dropped it when he went into the water to rescue the boy."

Tank could feel his feet sliding further down the bank. He stuffed the newspaper as far as he could into his shorts' pocket and then quickly grabbed the branch with his right hand too.

"Grab my hand," said Red, who was a little further up the bank and had wedged his feet between a couple of large rocks to anchor himself to the bank. Tank just could not get a firm footing, his feet were slipping further and further down the muddy bank.

"Hurry!" Red shouted as he held out his arm. Tank stretched up as far as he could and Red managed to just grab Tank's wrist pulling him a little higher up the bank. The extra lift helped Tank manoeuvre his feet on to the rock where Red was standing.

"That was close," said Tank as he pulled the newspaper out of his pocket and gave it to Red.

Red quickly unfolded it and looked at the front page. "Wow, it says 20 February 1946!" exclaimed Red. "It's 1946. Can you believe it?"

"Come on, we have to show the girls," said Tank.

With that both boys quickly retraced their steps back to the other two. It was hard to spot the girls from a distance as the dull brown of their outfits camouflaged them well with the greens and browns of the wooded bank. However, the girls were still in exactly the same place lying still, as Red had asked them to.

"Thank goodness you are all right," said Red, helping Fudge to her feet. He was relieved to see both of his cousins safe because Red was now able to see just how very steep this part of the bank actually was. "Well done, girls," he said.

"I was terrified," said Tiger. "We didn't know what had happened to you, whether you had gone in the water or been captured. It was horrible lying here not being able to see anything at all."

"We could hear voices, but we didn't dare look up," said Fudge.

"It was the gentleman and the Guard. They took the man away, a citizen's arrest they said for stealing the watch," said Tank.

"Which man?" asked Fudge.

"The one on the train, the one who was

reading the newspaper," replied Tank.

Tiger looked puzzled. "That man? But he seemed really nice."

Fudge was tugging on to Red's shirt. "What happened to the person in the river?" she asked. "Are they OK? Who was it? Was it that man? Who rescued him? Why aren't you two wet?" asked Fudge without pausing for breath or giving the boys any chance to answer.

"Slow down, Fudge," said Red as he gently removed Fudge's hand from his shirt. "We've got lots to tell you."

"You won't believe what we have seen," said Tank excitedly.

"Tell us," pleaded Tiger.

"We will tell you all about it," said Red. "There is just so much to say though. I suggest we find our way home first. We can talk as much as we want there. One thing we do know is that we could be in the year 1946."

"1946!" yelled Fudge.

"That's the date on this paper," said Red as he handed it to Tiger.

"Where did you get this?" she asked.

"Can't we just go home now, like Red said?" asked Fudge, not at all bothered about how they had found the paper. "I just want to go home."

"Fudge is right, we had better get a move on. Let's talk when we get home," said Red as he set off towards home.

Fortunately, there was no one else about so they could continue at quite a quick pace, not having to worry about keeping low or hiding behind trees. The path soon brought them out by the side of River View Cottage. The cottage still appeared empty. Not one of them suggested stopping to admire the pretty flowers or race pooh sticks though. They were all as keen as each other to get home.

"Over here," said Red as he walked to the side of the railway line. "Everywhere looks a little different in the woods. I think it is best we retrace our steps now on the railway track. Everyone follow me. Quick, let's get a move on while there are no trains," ordered Red.

They walked on a little until Tank

pointed up the hill. "Up there," he said, looking up the hillside. "It looks like there is a path up there. I think that could be our path home."

"I'm not totally sure," replied Red. He was not certain it was the path. He thought it looked familiar though and it was in about the right place. Red was a little annoyed with himself that he had not spotted the path. He usually knew the Trail like the back of his hand, but being on the railway line gave everything a completely different perspective. Red was quick to congratulate Tank though for possibly having found their way home.

The children kept a brisk pace as they walked up the hill, all spurred on by the thought of soon being home. As they were approaching the top of the hill, Fudge turned around and looked at the others. She had an enormous smile on her face.

"Look what I can see," she announced as she stepped to the side.

Red, Tank and Tiger looked ahead, all of them immediately thrilled to see the familiar sight of the beautiful little hamlet and their house just a little further down the road.

"Hooray, home sweet home!" shouted Tank as he sped off.

Fudge was close behind, calling for her Auntie Susan as she ran along the road.

Tiger hesitated. She turned to Red. "I've just had the most horrible thought," she said. "Something tells me that it can't be this easy, Red. Look at us, look at our clothes. How can we be home if we are still in the year 1946?"

Red was speechless. He felt his heart sink. Tiger was right. Surely it couldn't be this easy. Red hoped Tiger was wrong and he would just have some explaining to do to Mum about their different outfits. However, he suddenly had a very bad feeling about this too.

Red and Tiger looked up the hill and saw Tank and Fudge still quickly making their way towards the boys' home.

"If we're not home, then... where are we?" asked Red.

He did not wait for Tiger to answer. Both of them did not have to say another word. They simply ran as fast as they could to catch up with Tank and Fudge before they went into the house.

Red and Tiger were only a few metres away when they saw Tank just about to go into the front garden. Tank went to open the latch of the front gate, but he suddenly stopped.

"Tank!" shouted Fudge as she ran into the back of him.

Tank turned around and looked at Fudge. Red and Tiger were just behind her now too. Tank looked exceptionally pale, the colour having drained from his previously rosy cheeks.

"This is bad," announced Tank. "I don't think we are home."

They all stared at the unfamiliar man outside the front door. He was sitting on a little wooden stool and wiping his hands with a dirty rag. He leant over with a painful groan, dropped the dirty rag on the floor and picked up a little china cup and saucer by his side. As he took the cup off the saucer and raised it to his mouth, he saw the children and scowled.

As Red pulled Tank backwards away from the gate, he muttered, "Tank's right. We are not home!"

Chapter 8

Homeward bound?

The children were shocked and still staring at the man in the garden. Red could see now that the house looked a little different. The front door was black, not white, and the paint was peeling a little. Also, Red could not see the two baskets of flowers that usually hung each side of the front door. Mum and Dad did not have time to do much gardening, but Mum's hanging baskets were often the talk of the hamlet.

"We're looking for Auntie Susan," answered Fudge as she stepped a little nearer to the gate. "She lives here."

The man stood up off his stool and snapped at Fudge, "You won't find a Susan here. I have lived here all my life and there is no one of that name in this hamlet."

"Are you sure?" asked Fudge. "I want Auntie Susan," she said as she turned and nestled her head against Tiger's chest. Tiger took Fudge's hand and led her away from the man and the house back towards the track.

"Where are you going?" asked Red.

"None of this makes sense at the moment," said Tiger, waving the newspaper above her head. "You have still got to tell us what happened with the newspaper man by the river. The only thing I am certain of is that everything was fine until we went down the tunnel this morning. I'm going to go back up the tunnel now. It's got to be worth a try, hasn't it?"

The children all agreed that Tiger's suggestion made perfect sense. They made their way back down the path towards the river. A short distance down the hill, Red stopped and looked around to get his bearings.

"I reckon this is our oak tree," he said as he tapped the trunk of an oak tree on the side of the path.

Tank looked up. "What, the one that marks the spot where the tunnel is?" he asked. "It can't be. It's not big enough."

"Of course it isn't, silly." said Red. "Think about it, Tank. If we are in 1946, then the tree is nearly fifty years younger than our oak tree we see every day."

"Oh yeah," replied Tank, nodding his head.

"Did you know that you can tell the age of a tree by counting the rings on the inside of the trunk?" said Red. "Dendr...," he paused and then continued, "Dendrology, yes, dendrology, that sounds right. Dad told me that is the word for the study of trees."

"You are clever," said Fudge.

"Well, not really," said Red. "I just like trees and plants and, well, the Trail generally. You were clever and quick thinking on the train with the tickets, Fudge, and you are clever trying to use big words all the time. Everyone is clever in different ways."

Fudge smiled. "I don't always get the words right though, do I?" she said. "I will remember that though, dendrology."

"We haven't got time for this!" shouted Tank impatiently, as he went off the track and dashed across the woodland.

"Where are you going?" Tiger called after him.

"To the tunnel, of course," Tank replied.

"Oh no, I am not going *down* there again," Tiger quickly interjected. "That is what may have got us into this trouble in the first place. I think we should come back *up* the tunnel from the entrance by the river. You know, reverse the journey we made this morning to see if it reverses what happened to us. So we go forward in time, I guess."

Red thought it a great plan. It made as much sense as it could in the circumstances. Tank huffed as he had to retrace his steps to re-join the others who were now running down the hill towards the railway track.

"All clear!" shouted Tiger, as the four of them ran across the line to the river bank.

"Oh no," said Red as he looked across the river and up to the brow of the hill. "Tanner's Farm is not there. How are we going to find the tunnel entrance without Tanner's Farm as one of our reference points? This may take some time."

"You're forgetting something, Red," said Tank as he looked up towards the sky.

"The sun. Really, Tank. Could you find it by using the sun as a reference?" asked Tiger, looking rather impressed. Red was curious too. What was Tank thinking?

"Come on, guys. It's up there," Tank said very smugly.

"We haven't got time for this. Tell us quickly, Tank," urged Red.

"The broken signal post over there," replied Tank. "The one that made the loud bang. That is where we first came up on to the track."

"Brilliant, Tank. Sheer genius," congratulated Red. "If we go down the bank from that point, then we are bound to be within metres of the entrance. What are we waiting for? Lead the way, Tank."

Tank proudly ran to the signal post and then sidestepped down the bank until he came to a mound of greenery.

"Over here," he said as he grasped a large clump of ivy in his right hand.

Red and the girls were standing close behind him now. Fudge actually had her fingers crossed as they waited for Tank to reveal what lay underneath the mass of ivy. As Tank slowly pulled the ivy to the side, the children were delighted to see the entrance to the tunnel revealed.

"Hooray!" shouted Red.

"Yippee!" shouted Fudge, punching her arms into the air with relief.

"Not that I want to ruin the party, but we're not home yet," said Tiger. The others knew she was right. They still had to go up the tunnel and see what happened. "Only one way to find out though, I suppose," she said as she clutched the newspaper with one hand and took Fudge's hand with the other, holding it ever so tightly indeed as they both entered the tunnel.

"I'm scared this time," said Fudge.

"Don't be. I have a feeling we are on our way home!" Red shouted ahead as he gave Fudge a gentle nudge in the back to make her go even faster. "Come on. We might as well run up and go for it."

Tank quickly repositioned the ivy over the tunnel entrance and then broke into a short sprint to catch up with Red, Tiger and Fudge.

It did not take the children any time at all to run up the tunnel. Tank did not stop to pick up sticks or play along the way. He was as determined as the others to reach the top as quickly as possible on this occasion.

Tiger and Fudge exited the tunnel first.

"Just what I wanted to see," said Red as he and Tank followed the girls out. Tiger and Fudge turned around to see Red studying his clothes. Tiger and Fudge looked at their outfits too. Tiger had never been so pleased to see Fudge in her pretty spotted dress. Tiger was just as thrilled to see that she was wearing her new jean dungarees again, not because it was her favourite outfit, but because surely this was a good sign, that they were home and back in the year 1995.

The four quickly hugged each other, thrilled to think that they would soon be back home.

As the children hurried along to join the path that led to the hamlet, Fudge cried out, "The oak tree! It's ginormous. That's a good sign isn't it?"

Red and Tank burst out laughing.

"What now?" asked Fudge.

"There's no such word as ginormous, silly. It is either enormous or gigantic," said Tank.

"Fudge is right," said Tiger, supporting

her sister. "Ginormous is a real word. It is a cross between giant and enormous and I am sure it is in the dictionary. We can look it up later, if you like."

Fudge did not need to say anything as Red and Tank looked a little embarrassed and Red quickly praised her for spotting the tree.

"It is a good sign about the tree, you're right, Fudge," he said. "It sure looks like our big oak tree. Home, here we come, I reckon."

"I can't wait to see Mum and Dad," said Tank. "Bet they are going to be mad with us though, we've been gone ages. How are we going to explain this?" he asked.

"Let's just get home first," said Red. "Leave the talking to me."

As the children ran up the path and through the hamlet towards their house, Red had an awful feeling of *déjà vu*. He wanted to see Mum and Dad more than ever, and certainly not that cross man sitting on his stool.

Tank confidently led the way through the gate to the front door. Red was reassured by the familiar bright orange and yellow flowers cascading down from the two hanging baskets. "Mum's baskets," he thought.

Tank opened the door, but then stopped just as he stepped into the hallway. "You go first, Red," he said as he turned and looked at his brother.

"It's all right, Tank. We're home, I'm sure of it," said Red, passing Tank and leading the way towards the kitchen.

"Is that you, Red?" they heard Mum call from the back of the house. Red breathed a sigh of relief and entered the kitchen.

"What's going on?" asked Mum as she stared at the four of them.

"Sorry we're late, Mum, but...," Red started to say.

"Late?" interrupted Mum. "You have only been gone twenty minutes."

"Twenty minutes," said Tank.

"Yes, it's not even nine o'clock yet. Have you forgotten something?" she asked.

The children looked at each other, not quite sure what to say.

"Yes, the watch," replied Tiger. "I couldn't find the watch, Auntie Susan."

Mum looked a little worried. "You haven't lost it already have you, Tiger?" she asked.

"No, it's just that, well, I thought it was in this pocket and, well, er…," Tiger paused as she put her hand in her dungaree pocket to show her Auntie Susan it was empty. However, as her hand reached further down, Tiger could feel the cold metal of the pocket watch against her fingertips. "It's here, I actually have the watch!" she squealed as she pulled it out.

Mum raised her eyes. "Honestly, children. You would forget your heads if they weren't screwed on," she said as she picked up her handbag and keys and made her way to the front door. "Well, happy researching and see you later in the shop," she added, just before the door closed behind her.

"Unreal!" was all Red could manage to say, as he sat down at the kitchen table and stared at the clock directly in front of him. Forty-one minutes past eight. They had only been gone twenty-one minutes.

"Was it just a dream?" asked Red.

Tank bent down and studied the fresh cut on his leg. It still felt very tender. "It was real all right," said Tank pointing to his wound.

"Ouch! How did you do that?" Tiger asked.

"Red did it. He threw me to the ground," said Tank.

"That's so not fair, Tank," said Red. "I didn't throw you. I pulled you down so we did not get caught. I was protecting you."

"Protecting? Some protecting," said Tank sarcastically.

Tank, Tiger and Fudge joined Red at the large rustic oak table. Tiger scrutinised the watch carefully before placing it down on the table in front of them.

"It is definitely the same watch," she said, as she looked at the writing on the back. "How on earth did that get back in my pocket? It was not there when I came back up the tunnel."

"You're right," said Tank. The last we saw of the watch was when the man gave it back to the gentleman."

"Oh, do tell us all about it," said Tiger. "We still don't know what you saw. All we know at the moment is the man with the newspaper was taken away for stealing the watch."

Red paused. "It's all a little confusing. I still haven't quite worked it out myself. Let's see. First things first, it was the man with the newspaper who saved the boy from drowning in the river. Tank and I did not need to help as we got there just as the man was pulling the boy out of the water. We hid out of sight, but we saw everything."

"Was the boy all right?" asked Fudge.

"Yes, and guess what? The boy was actually the smartly-dressed boy from our carriage," said Red. "The one with the neatly gelled hair."

"The boy ran away though, just after the man had saved him," added Tank.

"Ran away? That's strange," said Fudge. "Why would you run away from someone who had just saved your life?"

"Well, it gets even more curious," said Red. "When the boy ran away, the man picked up the pocket watch off the floor. That is when the gentleman and the Guard found the man and said he was the thief. The man took the blame."

"So, the man stole the watch from the gentleman in the train?" asked Fudge.

"I don't think so," replied Red. "Well, it all happened so quickly, but it looked like the watch had fallen out of the boy's jacket when he ran away. That's right, isn't it, Tank?" asked Red.

"I think so," replied Tank. "The boy picked his jacket up so quickly that the watch fell out. I don't think the gentleman and the Guard saw the boy though. They weren't there then. They just saw the man holding the watch, which is why they thought the man was the thief."

"What you say doesn't make sense though," said Tiger. "Why would the man take the blame if it was actually the boy who had stolen the watch? Why not tell the gentleman that the boy had in fact stolen the watch and had just run away into the woods?"

"Well, this is where the plot thickens," continued Red. "You see, the man seemed to know the boy. He called him by his name. What was it? Um, Richard I think. Yes, I'm sure that was it."

"Gosh. So, if the man knew the boy, do you think they were working together?" asked Tiger.

"Accomplices," said Fudge confidently.

"Accomplices. That's a really good word, Fudge," Red said, smiling at his little cousin.

"There was something strange about how the boy appeared from nowhere when he first came into the carriage," said Tiger. "He had not been waiting on the platform with us."

"Yes, and when he was getting off he pushed past me to get to the train door first," said Red. "He had probably just grabbed the watch and wanted to get off the train as quickly as possible, to make his getaway into the woods."

Red paused a little as he recollected what else he had witnessed. "Mind you, the man was in no rush to get off the train, was he?" he continued. "He was the last person to get off. He was not even with the boy. They weren't sitting together on the train and they did not speak to each other at all. So it didn't look like they were working together."

"Yes, but that's probably all part of the act, isn't it?" said Tiger. "Perhaps the man tells the boy what to steal before they get on the train, they pretend not to know each other when on the train and then they meet up afterwards, after the deed is done, for the man to collect whatever the boy may have stolen."

"Yes, but in this case the boy fell into the water," said Red. "I reckon that perhaps the boy was hiding on the bank, waiting to meet the man at their secret meeting point in the woods, when he slipped and fell into the water. The bank was really slippery, wasn't it?"

"It was really, really slippery," said Fudge, chuckling to herself. "I should know, I nearly went for a swim myself!"

"It's good that we can laugh about it now, but it was scary at the time," said Tank.

"What if the man is in charge of lots of children and he makes them all steal for him?" said Fudge.

"What, like Fagin in *Oliver Twist*?" joked Red. "That may be a bit over imaginative Fudge."

"We did not see any other children, did we?" Tiger said to her sister.

"You never know though," said Red. "What if he is a well-known criminal from the past? Perhaps that is why he looked so familiar. Gosh, what if he is so well known that he uses the newspaper to hide his face from the other passengers."

"The newspaper!" exclaimed Tiger. "I don't have it any more. I was carrying it in the tunnel. I don't remember having it when I came out."

"We're forgetting one important thing," said Tank. "The man can't be that horrible. He saved the boy from drowning, didn't he?"

"Of course he saved the boy," said Tiger. "The boy would be no good to him dead. The boy was also carrying the watch. Perhaps he had other valuables on him too that the man did not want to lose in the water."

"Also, you said that the boy ran away before the gentleman and the Guard arrived. If no one knew about the young boy stealing for the man, then that is probably why the man kept quiet about him. I suppose he would have got into even more trouble with the police if he had revealed to them that he was using the young boy to steal for him."

"Gosh, to think we not only travelled back in time but we shared a railway carriage with a criminal," said Fudge.

"I don't think any of us really quite believe it yet," said Red. "Look, I suggest we keep quiet about the tunnel and the watch at the moment, at least until we have done some research and we know some more. Everybody agree?"

Tank, Tiger and Fudge all looked at each other and nodded.

"Right, let's start again. To the library everyone, and I suggest no detours down tunnels this time!" said Red, grinning.

"I'm starving, I need to eat first," said Tank. Seems like I haven't eaten for a day, even though we had breakfast not long ago."

⸺⸕⸻

Red grabbed some cartons of juice and a packet of custard creams from the kitchen cupboard. They would eat them on the way to the library as there was no time to waste. They had even more research to do now. They needed to find out about this watch and just who this criminal was who they had shared a railway carriage with!

Chapter 9

Headline news

The library was deserted, except for a man studying a book in the fiction aisle and Miss Burns, the librarian, who was neatly placing the daily newspapers in the display rack by the front desk.

"Great! Let's go set up in that corner," said Red, pointing to the empty seats and desks at the far end of the library. "It is usually quiet in that study area. We can also use both of those computers for our research."

Red and Tiger pulled up their chairs in front of one desk and Tank and Fudge sat at the other.

"Shall we have a competition to see which team finds out the best information?" suggested Red.

"That's so not fair," said Tank, crossing his arms in front of him. "Fudge and I are the youngest; you two are bound to win."

"Perhaps best we don't make it a competition," said Tiger diplomatically. "Let's work together. How about I come over there with you, Tank? We can find out about the date we travelled back to and criminals of that era. Perhaps Fudge and Red could research the pocket watch a little."

"OK," said Tank, as he unfolded his arms and gave Tiger the cutest dimpled smile in appreciation.

"I'm going to go and find an antiques book containing pictures of pocket watches," said Fudge, as she marched in the direction of the non-fiction section.

"Great! See you then, partner," Red called after her whilst waving goodbye.

Red hedged a bet with Tank and Tiger that Fudge would get side-tracked in the children's corner.

"I bet she comes back with a novel to read and forgets all about bringing an antiques book back," joked Red.

Tank was laughing too, but Tiger was too busy, already intently looking at her computer screen. She was clicking on the newspaper archive icon on her computer when Miss Burns walked by.

"Hello, children. If you need any help, just ask," said Miss Burns, as she peered over the top of her glasses at Tiger's computer. "It's an easy system," she said and then quickly explained to the children that if they knew the date of the newspaper they were looking for, they could simply type that date into the search button at the top of the screen. Otherwise, they could just browse through the different papers.

"Thanks, Miss Burns," said Red.

He liked Miss Burns a lot. She was always kind to the boys when they went into the library. The boys would occasionally pop in to take shelter if they were caught in town in an unexpected hailstorm or torrential downpour. However, no matter what state Red and Tank turned up in, usually muddy or soaked to the bone, Miss Burns always warmly welcomed them into her perfectly kept library. The boys would sit in the children's corner reading books and studying the posters on the wall until they had either dried out a little or the storm had passed.

Red and Tank both thoroughly enjoyed

the time they spent in the library and, one stormy afternoon, they actually taught themselves Morse code. The boys had then been asked to do a demonstration about it in a school assembly when their head teacher had found out about their unique skill.

Miss Burns knew the boys, as she would often see them on the Trail when she walked Misty, her cute little Yorkshire terrier. Tank would always stop to stroke Misty's coarse white fur.

Tank loved dogs and both he and Red longed for one of their own. Tank dreamed of walking a bouncy, chocolate Labrador that he would call Betsy or Bertie. Red loved collie dogs and also liked both of the names Tank had suggested.

Dad had told the boys last Christmas that they would think about getting a dog when either Mum or Dad were at home more. They were hoping to get a new member of staff to help them in the shop soon and, just as soon as they did, Dad had promised the boys a trip to the Dog Rescue Centre, to see if there was a 'bundle of love they could rehome', as Dad had so nicely put it.

Tiger pulled her chair in closer to the computer and raised her hands above the keyboard to type, poised just as if she were about to play a tune on a piano.

"What was the exact date you mentioned, the one on the newspaper?" she asked.

"20 February 1946," Red quickly replied, before Tank even had time to think.

Tiger typed in the date and pressed the button. The three of them sat in suspense waiting for the blank screen to change before their eyes. The library was silent apart from the loud, whirring noise of the computer.

"It's working its magic for us," Tiger whispered.

The three of them were huddled together all staring intently at Tiger's screen when Tiger cried out "Bingo!" as a mass of writing filled the page.

"Ssshh, Tiger," said Tank sniggering. He found it funny that Tiger was the one who had forgotten herself and shouted out so loudly. It was so unlike Tiger.

"Gosh, look at how many different newspapers are actually listed," said Tiger as she scrolled down the list. "Can anyone remember which paper it was?"

"I can't," replied Tank, shrugging his shoulders.

"Neither can I," said Red. "I don't remember seeing the name of the newspaper at all. I was too busy trying to check out the date."

"How about I put in more information?" said Tiger as she typed in Cornwall.

Within seconds, the long list of newspapers reduced dramatically.

"Still loads to choose from," she said rather disappointedly as she looked at the computer screen. "It will take us ages to look at each paper on this list."

"Just type in a smaller search area, like Bodmin or Wadebridge," suggested Tank.

Tiger typed in Wadebridge first and two papers appeared. *The Wadebridge Standard* and *The Camel Post*. Tiger quickly clicked on the first paper.

"What are we looking for?" asked Tank as they stared at the front page of *The Wadebridge Standard*.

As Tiger clicked on the second paper, the front page of *The Camel Post* appeared.

"That's it!" cried Red, jumping out of his seat in excitement. "That's the front page of the paper the man was holding on the train. I remember those headlines, 'Train Derailed in Padstow' and that photograph of the steam train that took up the whole page. Yes, I can just see the front page clearly now. Do you remember, Tiger?"

"I remember, Red. Yes, that is the paper," said Tiger. "You see, Tank, the first thing this shows us is that the newspaper the man had on the train, the one you found, actually did exist. There is no way we could all just have imagined this."

"So, it looks like we did travel back to 20 February 1946," said Red.

"I reckon that if we trawl through these local newspapers for a few days or more after this date, it may say what happened to the man with the newspaper who stole the watch. You know, a court report or something like that," said Tiger.

"Gosh, that is a clever suggestion! Where did you get that idea from?" asked Tank, looking at his cousin with admiration.

Tiger had a real passion for reading and

puzzles in general. "Must be from one of the books I have read," she replied.

"Well, we may not find anything, but it's certainly worth a look," said Red. Tank nodded.

"How about you log on to your computer too, Red, and we can each read a paper from a different day," suggested Tiger. "That way, we can get through them more quickly."

Red did as Tiger said and started reading the newspaper dated 21 February 1946. Red took his time looking at the photographs and really digesting the interesting stories. He was absolutely fascinated reading about the farmers' markets taking place, the price of coal going up, the fire that had started in a nearby baker's and about the new businesses opening in town. One article even mentioned Mr Jolley's sweet shop. Red felt like he was having his own private history lesson right here in the library. He could picture every event even more vividly now, probably because he had experienced a little snapshot of life in the 1940s on the train ride.

"I think you need to speed up, Red," said Tiger as she opened up her fifth newspaper. Red was still reading the same one. "You don't need to read every article in depth. I am just reading the headlines and the title for each article to see if that says anything about the thief. If it doesn't, then it is not worth reading," said Tiger ever so helpfully.

"Oh, right," Red said, a little embarrassed by the fact that he had got completely immersed in each article he had been reading. "I just never realised it could be so interesting sitting here and reading newspapers. I think I am going to start reading Dad's newspapers from now on. It's amazing what you can learn about different people and the area around us. Did you know, Mr Jolley's sweet shop actually opened in 1946?" he asked the others.

Tank looked shocked. "Really, I just thought it was made to look like an old-fashioned sweet shop," he said.

"See, look at Mr Jolley," said Red, pointing to his computer screen and the photograph of Mr Jolley standing proudly outside his sweet shop.

"That can't be Mr Jolley," said Tank

laughing. "He looks so different with all that hair."

"Mr Jolley wouldn't have been bald all those years ago, silly," said Red. "Anyway, this is the original Mr Jolley, the dad of the Mr Jolley we know."

"Well, that's all very good, but we really need to get a move on now," urged Tiger, glaring at Red to hurry up.

"You're right, Tiger," said Red. "Mum says I have the attention span of a goldfish. I must get a move on. Which paper shall I look at next?"

Tiger checked the date of the paper she was reading and told Red to read the next one.

As Red clicked the button for the paper dated 27 February 1946, he was not at all prepared for the headline that burst on to the screen in massive bold letters:

'HENLEY MANOR GARDENER STOLE POCKET WATCH!'

Chapter 10

What the newspapers say

Red quickly scoured the next couple of lines: *Today, at Bodmin Court, thirty-one-year-old Edward Meeks, admitted the theft of a pocket watch.*

"I've found it!" Red shouted out. "Where's Fudge? Fudge, come here!" yelled Red, forgetting for a moment that he was in the library.

"Ssshhh!" came a voice from behind them.

Peering around the end of the bookshelf of the fiction aisle was the man who they had seen when they first entered the library. He looked very cross and stared over at the three of them. Tutting loudly and shaking his head, he sidled back into the aisle.

Miss Burns glanced over from the front

desk, but she did not say anything to the children. The corners of her mouth turned up a little as Red held his hand in the air acknowledging his mistake. She quickly returned to stamping the books from the overnight deposit box.

Fudge suddenly appeared out of nowhere.

"Look what I have found, Tiger," she said, holding up a book. "It's that book we asked Mummy to buy us, about the princess and the unicorn. If Red could loan it out for me today, I will have time to read it before we go home on Sunday."

Before Tiger even had chance to reply, Red had a fit of the giggles.

"What is it?" asked Fudge innocently.

"Fudge!" said Tiger, giggling too.

"Red had a bet you would come back with a storybook for yourself and nothing at all to do with the watch research," said Tank. "That's why it is so funny, Fudge. Red was right."

"Perhaps I have just left the antiques book on the table over there," said Fudge, pulling a funny face at Red.

"Good try, Fudge, but that table is empty," said Red. "Anyway, never mind. Everyone, look at what I have found. This is it," announced Red as the four of them huddled around his computer, so they could all get a good view of the screen.

Red started to read the article out aloud, although not too loud so as to disturb the man who was now browsing at the books in the gardening section.

"*Today, at Bodmin Court, thirty-one-year-old Edward Meeks, admitted the theft of a pocket watch. Meeks admitted stealing the silver watch from George Grey.*"

"Stop reading a moment, Red," said Fudge. "It says Meeks. He has the same name as Mad Meeks."

"I know, what a coincidence it is the same surname," said Red. "Let me finish reading it all first though, and then we can go through the article in detail."

Red continued to read.

"*Both men had been travelling in the same railway carriage between Bodmin and Wadebridge. Grey noticed the watch missing just moments after Meeks had left the train. Thanks to the quick thinking of the Guard, and the patience of the other passengers, Meeks was caught red-handed in the woodland, just a short distance from The Shooting Range station."*

Red paused and took a deep breath before continuing.

"Grey informed the Court that Meeks had co-operated with a citizen's arrest and the watch had been returned. The Court heard how the watch had been a wedding present from Grey's wife and the couple had, in fact, been travelling back from honeymoon when the theft occurred."

"Wait," said Tiger, interrupting Red again. "Do you remember I said that the lady in the carriage looked like a film star, Red? It says here that she was travelling back from honeymoon with the gentleman, George. Perhaps that is why they were wearing such beautiful matching outfits."

Red agreed that this made sense, but he quickly started to read the rest of the article as he was anxious to complete it.

"PC Manners, heading the police investigation, informed the Court that had Grey and the Guard not carried out such a quick and thorough search of the surrounding woodland, Meeks would no

132

doubt have made it to the safety of his home and have avoided a citizen's arrest. He also informed the Court that, despite Meeks' confession when found, he considered Meeks' refusal to go into detail about the crime, or explain why he was drenched, very odd indeed. PC Manners suggested that Meeks may have been attempting to hide the watch in the nearby river bank and fell into the water as he was doing so, but this was pure speculation. Meeks declined to pass any comment to the Court other than to offer an apology for both the theft and any water damage caused to the watch.

Meeks was ordered to pay a £6 fine to Grey. The Court was aware that, as a result of the crime, Lord Pennington had already sacked Meeks as Head Gardener at Henley Manor. Meeks had been employed there for fifteen years, so it was accepted that losing such a longstanding and prestigious job was in itself a significant punishment to Meeks."

"My head's hurting," complained Fudge, as she put her head in her hands.

"It is a lot of information to take in," agreed Red. He suggested that they go through the article now line by line to try and make more sense of it. He slowly started to read the first sentence aloud again when Tank jumped up.

"Edward Meeks," said Tank. "It has to be. I bet that's Mad Meeks."

"Well, I thought the man with the newspaper looked familiar when I saw him getting off the train," said Red. "That could be why. That man could have actually been Mad Meeks, just…," Red paused as he started to count on his fingers.

Tank completed the maths for Red, "1946 was forty-nine years ago, Red, so Mad Meeks would have been forty-nine years younger," finished Tank. "This article says he was thirty-one years old back then. If we add on the forty-nine years to today's date, then that would make Edward Meeks eighty today. Mad Meeks looks about eighty now, so it's probably him then, isn't it?"

"See, Tank's great at maths," said Red proudly. "It does all add up, I agree, about the man being Mad Meeks. Especially as he was arrested just outside River View Cottage too and that is where Mad Meeks lives."

"Gosh, we have always said that Mad Meeks is bad, haven't we, Red?" said Tank. "We told Mum and Dad, but they didn't believe us."

"Well, we were right to stay out of his way though," said Red.

The colour drained from Tank's face. "Just think of all those times we were by his house," he muttered to himself. "What would he have done to us if he had caught us?"

"Well, he got that boy to steal the watch for him," said Tiger. "Just imagine if he had forced you and Red to steal for him too."

Tiger knew as soon as she had said it that she shouldn't have, as Tank looked very scared indeed.

"Don't say any more, you're really scaring me," said Tank. "What about the boy though? The article does not mention him at all."

Red quickly scanned the computer screen.

"It says that Meeks refused to offer any explanation about the theft," said Red. "So he must have continued to keep quiet about the boy's involvement. This is interesting, see this line here," Red said, as he put his right index finger against the computer screen. "It says Meeks' greatest punishment had been the loss of his job as Head Gardener at Henley Manor."

"Isn't Henley Manor a garden centre?" asked Tank.

"Well, there is Henley Manor the Mansion," said Red. "I think some of the gardens were sold off which now house Henley Manor Garden Centre. That's where Mum gets her hanging basket bulbs from. That isn't what I meant though. There's something else that's interesting about the reference to Henley Manor."

"I know," said Fudge, putting her hand up as if she were answering a question at school. "It says he was Head Gardener. That explains why Mad Meeks' garden is always full of beautiful flowers."

Red nodded. "It does explain his garden," he said. "However, just before the boy ran away Mad Meeks said something about contacting Henley Manor."

"What are you thinking, Red?" asked Tank.

"Well, it was like he was saying he was going to contact Henley Manor, perhaps for the boy," replied Red. "I'm thinking that the boy worked there too. As a butler or waiter perhaps, with the smart clothes he was wearing. So, perhaps the man was going to let them know that the boy could not go to work at Henley Manor that day."

"Yes, and if they worked together, that would explain why the man and the boy knew each other," said Tiger.

"That poor boy," said Red. "He was probably happy when Mad Meeks lost his job. It would have meant the boy no longer had to see him every day at work."

"Perhaps Meeks did not steal any more after that anyway," said Fudge.

"Fudge, are you forgetting what we saw yesterday?" said Red. "Remember that dodgy deal? Mad Meeks is still up to no good, I am sure of it. He got away with nobody knowing about the boy all those years ago. He obviously hasn't learnt his lesson. It's up to us to make sure that the police know what he has done."

"We can't say anything," said Tiger. "No one will believe us about the tunnel and how you and Tank saw what happened. They will think we are mad. I am all for telling the truth, but this happened so long ago, Red.

What good would it do anyway?"

"Well, we should at least tell Mum and Dad and the police about the dodgy deal we saw Mad Meeks doing yesterday," said Red. "Someone has to stop him. What if someone else gets hurt otherwise?"

"We have no evidence though," said Fudge.

"What if he comes after us for telling on him too?" questioned Tank. "I really don't think we should get involved."

"But we are involved. We already know too much," replied Red. "Mum and Dad are always telling us to stand up for what is right and to face difficult situations head on. I really believe that we should at least tell the police about the money and the man stashing away items in his sports car. The police would want to know that."

"It's not much for the police to go on. It would be better if we had the car number plate," said Fudge.

"What a great idea, Fudge," said Red, patting his cousin on the back. "Let's quickly head over to Mad Meeks' now. We won't hang around. If the red sports car is there, then we can scribble down the number plate. Who knows? There may be other clues or we might see something else suspicious going on. It is worth a try, just to give the police as much information as possible."

Tank could not quite believe what his brother was suggesting.

"Back to Mad Meeks'? That's mad, isn't it? What if he is there?" he said, wincing at his brother.

"We need him to be there to get the information," replied Red. "Don't worry everyone. We have always outrun Mad Meeks before. He can't even walk very fast, so he is not really going to catch us, is he? Look, trust me. I will look after us all. Let's go then," said Red as he got up from the desk.

"I'm in," said Tank, standing beside Red.

Tiger and Fudge got up and started to follow the boys out of the library, but Fudge stopped just for a moment and turned around. She looked longingly at the *Princess and the Unicorn* book that she had left on the computer desk.

"I *so* want to borrow that book, Tiger," Fudge said to her sister. "I really hope we will be back later."

"I hope so too," said Tiger, quietly under her breath. "I really hope so too."

Chapter 11

Meeks exposed

"I have the biggest butterflies in my stomach ever," moaned Fudge, as the four of them jogged towards Mad Meeks' cottage.

"It's probably just a stitch," explained Red, stopping to catch his breath. The four of them had been going at a fair pace non-stop from the library to the junction of the dirt track that led up to Red and Tank's house.

"We could always go and fetch our bicycles now," suggested Tank. "I think I would feel a little safer as Mad Meeks would have far less chance of catching us then," he said.

"Look, he may not even be at his house," said Red. "Besides, even if he is, he wouldn't be able to catch us. He limps and he uses a walking stick. Even you should be able to outrun him, Tank!" joked Red.

"That's not fair. I'm the fastest in my class," said Tank defensively.

"I think Tank may be right about the bikes," said Tiger. "What if that tall man in the red sports car is at Mad Meeks' again? What if he is a fast runner? We may not be able to run away quick enough."

"Look, no one is going to catch us," replied Red. "If anyone is there and we are spotted, we just make a run for it. As long as we stay together we will be fine. There is no point going home and getting the bicycles now, that is just wasting valuable time," said Red.

Red quickly sprinted off towards River View Cottage. "Follow me!" he shouted, as he turned around and gestured for the others to catch up with him.

They did not have any choice now but to follow, unless they were prepared to let Red go on his own, of course. Tank, Tiger and Fudge looked at each other.

"Come on. It's best we catch up with him," said Tank, running after Red.

Tiger and Fudge weren't far behind, as they watched Tank sprint as fast as he could.

Tank was an incredibly fast runner and he actually caught up with Red. Tank even managed to run past Red, pulling a funny face at him as he ran alongside.

"How can Tank joke at a time like this?" asked Fudge.

"I don't know, but there is no way I'm running that fast on the way," replied Tiger. "I'm reserving my energy in case we need to make a quick getaway."

Tiger could see her remark had scared Fudge even more than the boys' comments.

"Look, Fudge. I think the boys are a little scared too, just like us," said Tiger. "They're just trying not to show it. Red's right though. If we all stay together, we will be fine. Have I ever let you get into trouble before?"

Fudge smiled at Tiger. "I'm OK," she said, as she and Tiger jogged a little quicker towards the boys.

Red and Tank were huddled together on the grass verge at the side of the Trail, waiting for the girls to join them.

"Everyone good to go?" asked Red, as soon the girls joined them and without giving them any time at all to rest. Tank, Tiger and

Fudge nodded in agreement though and, as the four of them ventured a little further, they could see River View Cottage nestled in the wooded river bank.

—∞∞∞—

It was always a place of mixed emotions for Red and Tank. Laughing over a game of pooh sticks one minute and then fleeing at the sight of Mad Meeks banging on his window the next. The boys never usually knew what to expect as it depended on whether Mad Meeks was at home.

However, today, Red felt a real shiver down his spine as he stared at the little brick cottage. There was no way Red was going to tell the others what he was feeling though, as he was clever enough to know that they did not need much excuse to turn around and go home. "Be strong," he thought, as he slowly walked towards the property.

The children did not speak at all as they approached. Tiger stayed protectively close to Fudge, both of them concentrating to make sure they copied exactly what the boys did.

First, they crept incredibly slowly towards the back garden wall. As they drew closer, Red and Tank crouched down on the grass verge just by the side wall, which led to the front of the cottage. Tiger and Fudge did the same and knelt on the grass beside the boys.

"There might be no one home, but we just can't take any chances," whispered Red.

"We look suspicious. What if someone comes by?" asked Tiger.

"We could say we are looking for our ball," suggested Tank.

"Excellent idea. Good thinking, Tank," said Red, giving his brother a congratulatory thumbs-up.

"What's the plan?" asked Fudge.

"I suggest that just I run to the front garden," said Red. "I can check if the red car is there and, if it is, I will get the number. You all stay here to start with, just in case Mad Meeks is about."

"Suits me fine," said Tiger, breathing a huge sigh of relief. "I am quite happy to wait here."

"I'll go," said Tank. "Let me do it, please Red."

"I don't think so, Tank. It's dangerous. It's best I go," replied Red.

"It can't be any more dangerous than waiting here," said Tank. "Besides, I am the quickest," he boasted and quickly jumped to his feet.

Tank had gone quite a way along the wall before Red even had a chance to stand up.

"Wait, Tank," Red quietly called after him. Red did not want to shout as he did not want to attract attention to the four of them. He was slightly annoyed that Tank had gone against his advice, but he was also extremely proud of his brave little brother. "He can be so determined," said Red proudly. "Let's just hope he does not do anything wild and reckless though."

"Come back quickly, Tank," urged Fudge quietly, probably too quiet for Tank to hear as he had already made his way to the end of the wall.

Tank carefully peered around the corner of the wall to get a good look at the front of the cottage. There, on the side drive was the shiny, red sports car. Tank's heart felt like it had missed a beat as he saw it. It was good the car was there, but Tank knew he had to be careful as this meant that the tall man was somewhere nearby.

Unfortunately for Tank, the car had pulled up so close to the front of the property that Tank had no choice other than to venture out in full view of the front of the cottage to be able to read the rear number plate. "There's only one thing for it," thought Tank. He needed to make a run for the river bank, so he could take cover there. From there, he could get the registration plate and see if anything else suspicious was going on without Mad Meeks or the tall man spotting him.

Tank could not see anybody in the car and the front gate leading to the cottage door was closed. Hoping the coast was clear, Tank quickly dashed across the front garden and towards the river bank. He made it past the car and then hurled himself on to the top of the bank.

Tank had been a little over zealous in his bid not to be seen and landed awkwardly on his left ankle. "Ouch!" he yelped as he felt a sharp pain in his foot. Tank had a quick glance down, but he could not see any cuts or grazes on his skin. However, the sharp, shooting pain Tank felt in his ankle really was quite unbearable. Tank knew he had to put it to the back of his mind though and concentrate on the task in hand.

He looked up and saw the number on the plate of the car. "RP1. At least that's easy to remember," Tank muttered to himself.

Red, Tiger and Fudge were still kneeling down on the grass verge waiting for Tank to reappear.

"What's keeping him?" Tiger whispered.

Red looked towards the front of the cottage, but there was still no sight of Tank. Red shrugged his shoulders and, as he was about to say something, he stopped and listened.

"Voices," he said and pointed to the wall.

The noise was muffled at first but the voices became louder and louder. Soon, the three of them could make out that there were two men just on the other side of the wall.

"The boot's crammed full and ready to go," said a man.

"I am just going to get the boys first," another replied.

"Well, be as quick as you can. We don't want them dying on us," said the first man.

Red, Tiger and Fudge looked at each other in horror. "They mentioned someone dying," whispered Fudge. "I'm really, really scared, I want to go home."

"Stop talking or they may hear us," Red whispered back.

"We can't leave, Fudge," said Tiger, putting her arm around her sister. "We're not leaving until Tank's back."

"Tiger's right," said Red. "We must warn Tank about the men though, and that others may be coming here soon. We need to get him back here now," said Red.

"I'll go and get him," said Tiger bravely.

However, just as Tiger got up the children heard the loud clanking of a metal bolt.

"I won't be long!" they heard one of the men shout, followed by a loud, creaking noise.

"That sounds like it's the side gate opening," said Red.

"Oh no!" said Tiger, as she quickly knelt back down and buried her head in her hands. "What if they see Tank? What will they do with him?"

"Don't think like that. Tank can look after himself," Red reassured Tiger, as he discretely crossed his fingers and hoped his little brother would be fine. "Let's wait a couple of minutes and see what happens. I can't go yet as I might get caught," said Red.

<hr />

The children were still waiting when they heard a female call out on the other side of the garden wall. "Ted, I've made some lemonade. Do come and sit down."

"There's a lady there too," whispered Fudge. "I wonder who she is."

Tiger very carefully got up off her knees and raised herself up so the top of the wall was level with the top of her head. Very slowly, Tiger moved up and peered over the top of the wall. She could see a young lady sitting at a metal garden table, just outside the back door of the cottage.

She was young, perhaps about twenty-five or so. Her hair was scraped back into a neat ponytail and she was wearing a pair of very large sunglasses. She had a fantastic fuchsia-pink dress on, which matched the pinks of the flowers in the hanging baskets above her head. There was a large jug of lemonade and two glasses in front of her.

Mad Meeks then emerged from one of the greenhouses in the garden. Tiger watched as he started to limp towards the table.

"What can you see?" asked Red.

Tiger bent down and whispered, "Just Mad Meeks and a lady so far. Wait, I'll find out some more." Tiger stretched up again and peered over the wall. Mad Meeks was now sitting at the table next to the lady.

"The blooms are better than ever," said Mad Meeks, as he placed the secateurs and some freshly-cut lilies on to the tabletop. The lady poured him a large glass of lemonade and placed the glass in front of him.

"So, I heard Dad say he is doing the delivery straight after he has picked up the boys," said the lady to Mad Meeks, before taking a long sip of her lemonade.

"Yes. The car is loaded and ready to go," said Mad Meeks. "I really think he had better get a move on though. I'm not sure how long they will last in this heat."

"Dad won't waste any time getting the boys. He will be in and out in next to no time, like a military operation," said the lady laughing.

"They are talking about some kind of delivery and a military operation," Tiger whispered down to Red.

Red could not bear the suspense of waiting to have the information relayed from Tiger, so he too stood up to listen in on the conversation.

Fudge stayed kneeling on the grass verge because, even if she stood up, she would not be able to see over the wall. She wished at times like this that she was a little taller.

Mad Meeks pulled a large white handkerchief from his trouser pocket and used it to mop his brow.

"Thirsty work all this deadheading," he said.

Red gulped and looked over at Tiger.

"Deadheading," he said in her ear.

"I think he may mean the flowers. That is when you take the dead heads off flowers. I have helped Mummy do it," explained Tiger.

Red turned back to the garden to see the young lady gently place her hand on Mad Meeks' left forearm.

"Just think, Ted. How different things may have turned out if you had not done what you did to help Dad, all those years ago."

Mad Meeks frowned and put his glass down quite violently on the table. Red was surprised the glass did not break when it chinked against the metal.

"I take it then that your father has told you?" he asked. He looked furious. Tiger thought how much older he looked as his face crumpled and his wrinkles became even more pronounced.

"Yes, he has told me everything," she replied.

Mad Meeks banged his fist down on the table in a fit of anger.

"The fool! I told him never to tell a soul! To never speak of it again!" he bellowed.

The shouting scared Fudge. "Should we run away now?" she asked, jumping to her feet and tugging Red's shirt.

Red did not even look at Fudge. He was startled by Mad Meeks' reaction, yet, the suspense of not knowing what the lady knew was just too much. Red could not leave now, despite the fact that Mad Meeks looked like he was going to explode with anger.

"Not now," Red whispered, his eyes still fixed on Mad Meeks as he mopped his brow again.

Fudge did not dare to kneel or crouch back down. She stayed on her feet, facing the direction of Red and Tank's home, just in case Red or Tiger shouted 'run' at any moment. Fudge was well aware that she was probably the slowest of the four of them and that thought scared her immensely.

"Please don't be cross with Dad," said the lady to Mad Meeks. "We were reminiscing about Granddad and looking through the photo albums. I noticed there were no photographs of Dad with you. I thought it strange considering how close you are, well, how close we all are. I asked Dad why, and I could tell he was holding something back. I begged him to tell me all about you and him."

"I'm sorry, Penelope," said Mad Meeks. He rested his head in his hands and slowly wiped his face. He took a deep breath and, as he raised his head, Red and Tiger could see a strange calm had come over him.

"I did not mean to lose my temper, but it was just a shock, you speaking about it out of the blue like that," said Mad Meeks. "I told your father we should never talk about it again and, well, it all happened such a long time ago now."

The lady took Mad Meeks' hand. "I promise I will never tell anyone else," she said. "I just wanted to talk to you about it, while Dad is not here. To help me understand what happened that day and because, well, because you are like a Granddad to me too. I love you very much."

"I love you too, Penelope," said Mad Meeks as he smiled sweetly at the lady. "Now, tell me. What did your father tell you?"

"That you saved his life in more ways than one," said Penelope. "Dad told me that it all happened when he was fifteen, just a young lad and studying at the naval school in Plymouth. Dad said he loved his studies and he had hopes of being an Admiral one day."

Mad Meeks laughed. "Yes, have you ever heard anything so silly? An Admiral, and your father could not even swim back then."

Penelope laughed too.

"Sorry, I interrupted you," said Mad Meeks politely. "Yes, your father was at naval school. Do continue, Penelope."

"Well, Dad said some of the final year students had started to pick on him, calling him 'rich boy' and similar names," continued Penelope. "Dad thinks they were jealous that he lived at Henley Manor and that Granddad was Lord Pennington. The name-calling did not stop. In fact, Dad said things got even worse. The bullies demanded that Dad supply them with money. Dad felt he could not tell anyone about the bullies. He was scared, so he caved in to their demands."

"If only your father had told Lord Pennington or myself at the time," said Mad Meeks. "We would have helped your father and helped him deal with the bullies."

"That is one of Dad's big regrets," said

Penelope. "He says he felt so alone at the time, but he knows now that things would have been different if he had spoken up about it. Anyway, he didn't and that's why he got himself into the trouble he did. At first, Dad told me he had paid the bullies off with money from his trust account. When Dad ran out of money, he told the bullies but they still demanded more. Dad said he had actually considered selling some of the antiques from Henley Manor. However, he could not bear the thought of Granddad finding out that some of the family heirlooms were missing or, worse, Granddad may have wrongly accused one of the staff of stealing them."

The lady paused a little. "Dad said that, one day, he was so worried about the threats the bullies had made that he could not bear the thought of going to college. He was in his college uniform and ready to go but, on the spur of the moment, he just managed to jump on a train to Wadebridge. He had no plans to do anything but, then, as he was sitting on the train, right in front of him he saw a gentleman look at his silver pocket watch and, when he put it back in his pocket, Dad could see the silver chain hanging from the gentleman's waistcoat. Dad said that he doesn't know what came over him but, in an absolute moment of madness, he grabbed the watch and ran off the train. Dad felt awful. He could not believe what he had done and what he was going to do. It was then that he saw you, walking towards him on the path."

"I did not see him," said Mad Meeks. "I was making my way home. I was not feeling well that day, so Lord Pennington had given me permission to leave Henley Manor to go to the doctors."

"However, Dad had seen you and that is when he panicked. For a start, you would have known he was not at college when he should have been. Granddad would have been furious with that alone, and then there was the stolen watch to deal with. Dad said he had to quickly hide from you so he ran off the path and down the side of the river bank. It was steep and, as he hurried, he lost his footing and, well, you know the rest, he fell into the river. He thought he was going to die. The current was just too strong for him," said Penelope.

Mad Meeks sat forward in his chair. "I just remember hearing a cry for help. I saw a body in the water and, well, despite feeling very sick myself, I jumped in to save him."

"Gosh, to think Dad could have died if you had not risked your own life to save him," said Penelope.

"Anybody would have done the same," said Mad Meeks. "I did not know it was your father though, not until I got to the bank and carried him in my arms. I thought…," Mad Meeks paused. "I thought he was dead."

Mad Meeks leaned towards the lady and held her hand as he continued the story.

"I wanted to bring your father inside, to get him dry and well. He looked in a bad state. However, in a flash your father ran off into the woods. It was then that I found the pocket watch on the floor. At first, I thought it was your father's watch, as it had fallen out of his pocket. However, no sooner had your father run away when two men approached me and accused me of having stolen the watch. One of them told me that it was his watch for certain and referred me to a personal inscription on the back. I thought he was mistaken until I read the back of the watch. I did not know how and when your father had taken the watch, but it was plain to me at that moment that your father must have been in a great deal of trouble."

Penelope drew even closer to Mad Meeks. "That's when you took the blame for Dad, isn't it?" said Penelope.

"Yes," said Mad Meeks. "I cared for your father a great deal. I was working as the gardener at Henley Manor when he was born. I watched him grow up over those fifteen years into the fine young gentleman that he was. Your father and I had spent many an hour in the gardens together. He was such a sociable boy. Even at a young age, he would come and talk to me when I was potting plants in the greenhouse or weeding the borders. We had a bit of fun too. I can remember taking your father for rides in the wheelbarrow and having a quick game of cricket and football when your Granddad was not watching. Lord Pennington was a fine man, but he was a very busy man. He would spend most days either in his office or attending engagements. I suppose that's why I got to know your father as well as I did. Your father was like a son to me."

Mad Meeks squeezed Penelope's hand. "You must remember, your father had his whole life ahead of him," he said. "At the time, he had hopes of being an Admiral. He would have been thrown out of naval college with a police record. I feared your Granddad would have disowned your father too, had he found out. Any news of your father's theft would have disgraced Henley Manor and the reputation of the Pennington family, especially in Lord Pennington's social circle of judges and lawyers."

"I know how much you must have loved Dad," said Penelope. "You protected him, yet you lost absolutely everything. You lost your job and the respect you had within town. Still you never uttered a word to the police or to another soul."

"Your father came to see me the day after it had happened," said Mad Meeks. He wanted to confess all to the police and your Granddad. I urged him not to. I had already taken the blame and told the police

I had taken the watch. Your father had not asked me to do that. I just could not let him get into trouble and risk losing his title and career. I insisted. I loved him too much to see that happen to him. Your father was right though, we should have confessed. It is important to let you know that I have lived with this on my conscience every day since 20 February 1946. You see, I panicked. I so wanted to protect your father that I could not see what potential harm I was doing. I am ashamed of myself for not having told the truth and, quite frankly, I deserved to have been punished for that. Your father and I should have gone to the police, like your father suggested, and told them the truth. There would have been consequences for both of us, but I am sure your father would have been given some lenience because of those bullies."

"Yes, what happened to the bullies?" asked Penelope. "I forgot to ask Dad about them."

"He stood up to them and, when they realised your father had no more money to give, they left him alone. You see, bullies can be such cowards really."

Mad Meeks glanced down at his watch. "Where has Richard got to?" he asked.

"He has been a long time, hasn't he?" replied Penelope.

"I hope he comes soon as those blooms will wither up and die the longer they stay in that car boot. Henley Manor Garden Centre won't care if your father owns Henley Manor or not if he turns up with dead flowers to sell," said Mad Meeks. "Do you know? I don't know what I would have done financially had your father not sold my flowers for me each week. After losing my job and my income, your father actually saved me, in a financial sense of course. I found it hard to get another job, but your father visited me without fail every week. Each time he saw me, he took some of my plants and sold them for a good price. Originally, he sold them to different shops, but now the garden centre is attached to Henley Manor it makes it far easier for him. He has sorted out a nice little arrangement for me there. If your father had not done this for me, I would not have been able to afford living here years ago.

I would have lost my lovely home."

"Dad felt he had a debt to repay you," said Penelope. "It is more than that though. I know Dad loves you very much too. We all do." Penelope and Mad Meeks leant towards each other and embraced.

Tiger and Red crouched down a little. "Red, can you believe it? Mad Meeks was the newspaper man and he is really nice," said Tiger. "What a lovely story."

Red thought so too. They both knelt down next to Fudge.

"Everything is going to be all right now, Fudge," said Tiger, hugging her sister tightly.

"Where's Tank though?" asked Fudge.

"Tank!" said Red, suddenly remembering that Tank was still not back. "He's been gone ages. What on earth has happened to Tank?"

Chapter 12

Tank in a pickle!

Tank had been hiding on the river bank at the front of Mad Meeks' cottage when he had heard a loud, creaking noise followed by the thudding sound of footsteps.

Tank peeped through a hole in the bush and saw an extraordinarily tall man walking towards the car. Tank had not seen this man before, but Tank just knew straight away that it had to be the tall man the others had spoken about yesterday, the one who had been doing the dodgy deal with Mad Meeks.

Tank felt very uneasy as he watched the man walk towards the car. Fortunately, Tank had chosen the biggest bush to hide behind.

Tank peered as best he could around the bush to get as much information as possible about the man, as it was sure to assist the police if he could give them a detailed description.

"Baldish head, grey sideburns, wrinkled

face, dark top, dark trousers," Tank quietly reeled off to himself, just in case it would help jog his memory later on.

The man walked towards the boot of the car and was now exceptionally near to the bush Tank was hiding behind. If only he had quickly run out to the drive, got the number plate details and run back to the others, Tank knew he would not be in this pickle now.

Tank had to think fast. He wondered what Red would do in this situation. He closed his eyes for a second and tried to work out his best plan. The best he could think of was to simply remain hidden, just until the man had gone back inside the cottage or driven away. It was just far too dangerous to make a run for it.

Tank watched the man rummage in the boot, but he just could not get a good view of what was actually in the car. His crouched position restricted his view. Tank decided to attempt a quick knee shuffle manoeuvre to the other side of the bush.

As he clumsily shuffled a little to the right, he managed to take half the bush with him. The bush rustled far too loudly for

Tank's liking. He closed his eyes, praying he had not attracted the attention of the tall man. He felt his pulse racing unnaturally fast and his hands felt very clammy.

"Please go away," he muttered to himself, hoping the man had not seen him. He half opened his eyes and looked over to the car. The man was not there. Tank then opened his eyes fully and now he could see the tall man actually walking right towards the river bank, right towards where Tank was hiding.

"You boy! What are you doing?" shouted the man in a very gruff voice.

Tank was petrified. He jumped up to run away, but as he did he felt a sharp pain in his ankle and collapsed on the floor. Tank fell heavily and when he hit the ground everything became a bit of a blur...

Chapter 13

In the garden

Red was really worried now. He had not heard the car drive off and Tank had not appeared with the car number plate details. The lady and Mad Meeks were still chatting at the garden table.

"I'm going to go and find him," announced Red.

"Oh no. The tall man, he's got Tank," said Tiger, still peering over the wall to see the tall man walking from the other side of the cottage into the back garden, carrying Tank in his arms.

"Why is he not moving? What has he done to him?" asked Red.

Red did not stop to think. Without hesitation, he ran to the side gate and entered the back garden.

"Let go of my brother!" shouted Red at the tall man.

"Richard. What is going on?" asked

Mad Meeks, as he got up to look at the man holding Tank. "And who are you?" he asked as he turned to face Red.

Red puffed out his chest. "I'm Red. That's my brother. What have you done to him?" he bravely asked.

The tall man gently placed Tank on the floor.

"Quick, Penelope," he said. "Can you get an ice pack? I think he may have hit his head when he fell down. He was playing on the river bank and he seemed to fall very awkwardly. He seemed a bit dazed when I helped him up. I thought it best to bring him back here to make sure he is all right."

"Get the smelling salts too, Penelope! They're in the medicine cupboard!" Mad Meeks shouted towards the cottage.

"What's his name?" asked Mad Meeks.

"It's Tank," said Red.

"Tank. I like that," said Mad Meeks, smiling at Red. "Don't worry lad, your brother will be just fine."

Penelope came running out of the cottage with the smelling salts and waved them right under Tank's nose. Tank screwed up his freckled nose and turned away from the smell.

"He's all right," said Mad Meeks.

Red knelt beside Tank, placed his arm underneath his back and helped to raise him so he was nearly sitting upright.

"He's opening his eyes," said Red, still holding his brother in his arms.

"RP1," said Tank.

"Not now, Tank," whispered Red.

"RP1," Tank repeated.

"What's he muttering?" asked Mad Meeks.

"RP1, it sounded like," said Penelope. "That's your car number plate, Dad. How strange."

Red thought quickly. "Must have been the last thing he saw before he fell," explained Red. "Come on, Tank, no need to keep repeating that. You have had a nasty bump on the head," said Red, looking at the scarlet mark on Tank's forehead.

"Quite a shock you gave us all there," said Mad Meeks as Tank very slowly got to his feet. Tank looked worried as he looked at Mad Meeks and then at Red.

"It's all right, Tank. I'll explain it all later. Everything's going to be OK now," said Red. "It's best we get Mum to have a look at your head though. You have a right lump there. Probably banged it on a stone when you fell. What are you like, Tank?"

"My ankle's hurting too," said Tank as he bent down and rubbed his foot.

"He was in the bushes at the front, Ted, by the signs," said the tall man to Mad Meeks.

"You do look familiar, boys. Are you the boys who I see playing pooh sticks on the bank?" asked Mad Meeks.

"Yes, but please don't be cross with us," said Tank. "We're sorry if we have upset you."

"You haven't upset me," answered Mad Meeks. "I just worry about you when you play so near that river bank. The amount of times I have tried to talk to you boys. I have banged on the window to get your attention and sometimes I have come outside to talk to you. Yet, you always run away. I just wanted to let you know that this part of the river is so dangerous. The current is fast here and the bank gets very slippery when it is wet. I was worried in case you fell into the water. I'm too old to be rescuing you," he said. Red noticed Mad Meeks wink at the tall man.

"I even put the warning signs up in the front garden," he continued. They did not stop you kids though, did they?"

"We just thought you didn't like children or people playing near your house," said Tank.

"Tank!" exclaimed Red, shocked that his brother had been so bold as to say that.

Mad Meeks laughed out loud. "You couldn't be further from the truth," he said. "I love children. I have always loved children. I only wish I had children of my own."

Just at that moment two young boys ran into the back garden. They were cute identical boys with masses of blonde curls. They were about five years old, thought Red.

"Great Gramps!" the twin boys shouted out as they ran towards Mad Meeks. Mad Meeks bent down and hugged them.

"Hello, boys," he said.

Mad Meeks turned to Red and Tank. "Children, let me introduce you to Jamie and Bobby. These two are like great grandchildren to me. They are Penelope's boys. Penelope here is Richard's daughter. You may have heard of Richard Pennington. He owns Henley Manor," said Mad Meeks proudly.

"Mum always buys her bulbs from Henley Manor Garden Centre there," said Red. "Everyone says she always has the best hanging baskets."

The tall man, Richard, smiled at the boys. "Well, next time your Mum takes you there, how about you let me know and I will arrange for you all to have a cream tea in the restaurant?"

Penelope suddenly shot up out of her seat. "How did the boys get here?" she asked. "Dad, you were going to fetch the boys back from Helen's for me."

"I know, but I got side-tracked when I saw this young lad fall down," Richard replied. "We all forgot about picking up the boys after that," he said, looking at his watch.

With that, a young lady then appeared in the back garden with another little boy about the same age as the twins.

"Hi, Penelope," the lady called. "I hope you don't mind. I was worried when your dad did not turn up at my house to collect Bobby and Jamie. I knew you were visiting Ted, so I thought it best to make my way down here with them. The side gate was open; I saw them run straight into the garden."

"Oh, thank you so much, Helen, for bringing the boys back. Dad got side-tracked," Penelope replied.

Penelope asked the boys if they had had a nice time at Helen's, but they were far too busy to reply. Jamie, Bobby and their friend had all run off to hide in the garden. Mad Meeks had his hands covering his eyes and was counting, "I'm coming to find you," he said.

Mad Meeks turned to Red and Tank. "It was nice to meet you, boys. If you are ever passing, then please stop and say hello. I'm usually pottering around in the garden, so feel free to look over the wall. Here, take this bunch of lilies for your Mother," he said, offering Tank the freshly-cut flowers from the tabletop.

"Thank you," said Tank. "You are very nice."

Mad Meeks laughed again. "Just make sure you stay away from that river bank though. Promise me you will, boys?" he asked.

"We promise," Red and Tank said in unison before walking out of the garden.

Chapter 14
The end?

"We heard everything," said Fudge, as Red and Tank joined them at the side of Mad Meeks' cottage.

"We thought it best not to come into the garden though," said Tiger. "I couldn't believe it when I saw you actually being carried into the garden, Tank."

"Are you all right, Tank?" asked Fudge. "Did you faint?"

"No, I didn't," Tank replied, blushing a little. "I think I may have just knocked my head a little. I was only acting."

"Yeah, right," Red said as he hugged his brother, checking that he was feeling well enough to walk into town still.

Tank did have a bit of a headache and his ankle was hurting just a little now, but the thought of visiting Mr Jolley's made him feel a whole lot better.

Tank handed the bunch of lilies to

Fudge. "Here, Fudge. I know you like these flowers. You can hold them and give them to Mum, if you like."

"I just can't wait to see Auntie Susan. Mmm, they smell lovely," she said, taking the flowers off Tank and holding them under her nose.

The children walked ever so slowly along the Trail into town whilst they told Tank all about what they had overheard between Mad Meeks and Penelope.

"So, you're telling me Mad Meeks had absolutely nothing to do with stealing the watch? He didn't put the young boy up to it?" asked Tank.

"No. He loved the boy like a son. That is why he was selfless and took all the blame," said Tiger.

"And, guess what? The boy was Richard, the tall man who just helped you," said Fudge.

"No way!" said Tank. "What, the boy who stole the watch is now the owner of Henley Manor, and rich enough to have a sports car with a private number plate?"

"Yes. That's him. See, I got it so wrong, didn't I?" said Red. "I had thought the boy had worked at Henley Manor all those years ago, when in fact he was the future Lord of the Manor. It was only Meeks who had worked there as the gardener."

"So, Mad Meeks was the boy's garden angel," said Fudge.

"Fudge, you mean guardian angel," laughed Tiger.

"No, I actually mean garden angel," insisted Fudge.

Everyone laughed.

"Look, who agrees that we don't call him Mad Meeks any more?" said Tank. "It's just not a very nice name and, well, he is not mad, is he? He is actually really nice."

"You're right. He was lovely playing with Jamie and Bobby. We got him so wrong," said Red.

"It just goes to show that you should never judge someone by their appearance," said Tiger. "Mummy is always saying that. You know, never to judge a book by its cover."

"Shall we call him Kind Ted?" asked Tank.

"He is kind, but let's just call him Ted. That is his name, isn't it?" said Red.

"OK, Ted it is. It's a nice name too," said Tiger. "It's funny though, isn't it, how your imagination can get the better of you?" she said. "The fact that we thought they were doing a dodgy deal, yet all along Richard was doing a good deed for Ted. The boot was just full of flowers he was selling and the money we saw him paying Ted was obviously for the flowers he had sold."

"I know, and to think they were only talking about flowers and plants dying. We thought they meant someone was going to die, didn't we, Tiger?" said Red.

"That will teach us to eavesdrop," said Tiger. "Although, I suppose we would not have found out about how lovely Ted is and the truth behind the stolen watch if we had not carried on listening," she continued.

As the children approached Wadebridge, they were excited about seeing Mum.

"How are we going to explain about the tunnel and going back in time?" asked Fudge.

"We don't," said Red firmly.

"Why not? Shouldn't we tell the truth?" asked Tiger.

"Yes, but not just yet. I think we should just think this through first. I doubt Mum would believe us anyway," said Red.

"Bet you, if we told Mum, she would stop us going through the tunnel," said Tank.

"Worse than that, Tank," said Red. "She would probably stop us going on the Trail. We could be housebound all week!"

"Let's not say anything just yet. It could ruin our holiday otherwise," said Fudge.

"Who's to say it was the tunnel that was magic anyway? Perhaps it was the watch," said Tiger, pulling the watch out of her dungaree pocket. "Somehow, we went back in time to find out about the watch, didn't we?"

"I think you are right, Tiger," said Red. "Tank and I have been up and down the tunnel many times and nothing has happened to us before."

The children all looked at each other. None of them knew the answer. Not really, other than the journey back in time had been a real adventure.

"It is a mystery, isn't it?" said Red. "One thing is for sure though, I would not let the watch out of your sight until we are at the shop."

Tiger kept a tight hold of the watch all the way to town.

———

As they walked up the High Street they saw the familiar black and white shop front with 'This'n'that' in gold letters just above the windows. The bay window was crammed full of shiny and colourful objects.

The bell jingled as Red opened the door.

"Come on, Tank," said Fudge as she held the door open for him.

"I'm not allowed. Mum banned me after I broke all the antiques," said Tank, sulking.

Tank peered into the shop through the front window. He could see Red, Tiger and Fudge standing against the counter. Tank had his nose firmly against the glass trying to look for Mum.

"Hey, get your nose off my glass. You're leaving marks," said Mum who was standing in the shop door. Mum smiled at Tank. "Come on, I can hardly leave you outside when your cousins are here and when you have brought me these beautiful lilies, can I?" Mum held her arms wide open and, hugging Tank tightly, told him, "How can anyone resist that dimpled smile?" As Mum looked down at Tank, she obviously noticed the mark on his forehead. "Tank! What on earth have you done?" she asked.

Tank quickly pulled away. "Nothing," he replied.

"What am I going to do with you?" said Mum as she carefully ushered him to the counter, making sure he did not knock anything over on his way. "So, tell me what you know about the watch," she asked the children.

Mum was absolutely amazed as Tiger told her everything they had found out about the watch. Tiger was able to tell Mum that it was a gentleman's silver pocket watch that dated back to about 1946. It was purchased by Alice Grey as a wedding present for her husband George. Tiger told Mum that it needed to be professionally valued as it was a rare piece. It was actually made by a Cornish jeweller, Henry Priddy, and it was only one of ten that was made in this unique design.

Mum looked amazed. "Gosh, what fantastic research. Goodness only knows how you managed to find all that out in the library in just under an hour."

Red winked at the other three. If only Mum knew the adventure they had been on.

"Well, I think you have all jolly well earned your pocket money," said Mum.

Mum reached into her purse and pulled out a five pound note. "Each of you can buy a quarter of sweets. Be a dear, Red, and just pop the change back to me before you go home," she said.

As the children were leaving the shop, Fudge stopped and turned around.

"Oh, Auntie Susan, Tiger forgot to tell you how the watch was stolen in 1946."

Mum looked intrigued. "Goodness me, what is this that you have found out?" she asked.

Fudge did not have a chance to continue, as Tiger pulled her out of the shop.

"I don't know what she is talking about.

See you in a bit, Mum!" shouted Red as he closed the shop door.

No one needed to say anything to Fudge. She realised what she had said wrong. "Oops," was all she could muster as they walked across the cobbled street to Mr Jolley's.

<hr>

It did not take Fudge long to order her quarter of clotted cream fudge. Red and Tiger both opted for a quarter of pineapple chunks. Tank, on the other hand, was still studying the enormous selection of sweets. It took a while before he finally decided on the toffee bon bons and he cheekily managed to pop two in his mouth in one go!

"I'm so tired," said Red.

"It feels like we have been out all day and it is only half past eleven," said Tiger, as she looked at the clock on the Town Hall tower.

"Well, think how much we have done today. What an amazing adventure," said Tank.

"Yes, and to think this is only the first day of our holiday," said Fudge, as she took the last piece of fudge out of her bag.

"Fudge, you've finished your fudge already!" laughed Red, as he opened the door of 'This'n'that' to give Mum her change. Mum was just by the door adding a new item to the display.

"Ah, I'm glad you're all here. I've been thinking," said Mum.

"What is it?" asked Tank.

"Well, seeing what a great job you all did with the watch, I would like you to research *this* tomorrow morning," said Mum.

The children could not quite believe it. Red, Tank, Tiger and Fudge all looked at one another, and then at the object dangling from Mum's hand...

Tuesday

What was in Mum's hand and what would happen if they took it down the tunnel? Would it lead Red, Tank, Tiger and Fudge on another adventure?

Read *Tuesday*, the next book in the series.

Visit:

www.talesfromcameltrail.com

for more details.